Prowl

Nothing Else Matters but Survival

By

Deidra D. S. Green

Stephanie Nicole Norris

Note from the Publisher: This is a work of fiction. Any resemblance to actual persons living or dead or references to locations, persons, events or locations is purely coincidental. The characters, circumstances and events are imaginative and not intended to reflect real events.

Prowl

Nothing Else Matters but Survival

RATHSI Publishing, LLC and Love is a Drug Ink.

Acknowledgments

I am eternally grateful to the Creator of all things for every opportunity that he gives me for self-expression. The self that is being expressed is the self he engineered and I am awestruck at how much he loves me. My reading family has been with me since the very beginning. I appreciate you and want you to know that I never take your support, cheers, prayers, encouragement, willingness and love for granted. Thank you to my literary family. Rathsi Publishing Company is family and I love my family. Thank you to the members of Mahogany Writer's Exchange. You ladies help me in more ways thank you know. I appreciate you challenging me to be the best version of my literary self. Thank you to my writing partner on this project Stephanie Nicole Norris. Who knew that it would come to this? Thank you for the long brainstorming sessions, the planning sessions, the accountability, the laughs and the opportunity to come together to do something we both love.

Chapter One

Kunsthistorisches Museum
Vienna Austria

"Champagne madam?" Symone Ellis turned toward the server, a small smile hinting the corners of her lips.

"Danke," she said, thanking the man in his native German tongue. She removed a flute of the bubbly liquid from the sterling silver tray he held.

"And you, madam," the server said, balancing the tray effortlessly toward Drew Patterson, Symone's long time best friend. His accent was thick as if he'd never set foot outside of the country.

"Nein Danke," she declined.

The server moved off leaving the women to admire the 1617 painting of the decapitated head of Medusa, owned by Peter Paul Rubens, the greatest painter of Flemish Baroque. Leaning closer to Symone, Drew whispered, "We should've put this on our list."

Symone didn't bat an eye at the insinuation. Instead, she took a sip from her glass and puckered her lips like she was in deep thought before responding. "If you had it your way, everything in this museum would be on the list."

Symone stepped on to the next painting, pretending to admire its mastery.

To anyone who paid them any mind, Symone and Drew appeared to be two beautiful women that belonged to a heritage of money with the air of elegance they gave off. Draped in Valentino gowns that hugged their statuesque curves all the way down to the heels that accentuated their pedicured feet, the women exuded confidence and pedigree. No one would've known they were a part of an elaborate scheme to steal one of the museum's most prized possessions. Drew lingered in front of the head of Medusa a moment longer before gliding to Symone's side again.

"You guys should listen to me more often; my advice holds just as much weight as anyone else's."

Symone glanced at her. "Baby girl, what are you talking about? You're the brains of this operation."

"This time," Drew said. "But you guys should really take what I say into account more often."

"You really want to have this conversation now?"

Drew didn't respond, deciding to take this up with her sister Brooklyn and best friends later. The museum was crowded with the who's who from around the world. The highlight of today's feature was the introduction of a selection of art pieces from Peter Paul Rubens. Tomorrow would be the major exhibition honoring up to forty pieces of European art history. But none of it was what they came for. The particular treasure they wanted was behind the scenes, and today they were there to case the place. They'd laid all the plans out and studied them until they were a blueprint sketched in each of their minds' eye.

"Drew, not now. Stay focused." Her sister's voice chirped in the earpiece she wore.

Drew was not one to let things go, she had to get her point across. Being the youngest of the group, Drew felt disregarded most times. She swirled slow and elegant making eye contact with her sister Brooklyn across the room. Brooklyn was also beautifully dressed in a Vera Wang gown. Drew bit down on her teeth, crushing the retort that sat on her tongue. Next to her sister was another long-time friend, Leah Hunter; equally as gorgeous, showing off her long neck as her hair sat atop her head in a bundle of curls. Drew saw the smirk on Leah's face, knowing it was hard for Drew to follow orders without a snarky response.

“On the right,” Symone said sauntering toward the area that held the gem, smiling and nodding as she passed other attendees. Getting closer to the area she’d mapped out in her mind caused a sudden rush of excitement to flicker through her, but an image in her peripheral vision caused Symone to stop dead in her tracks. Symone didn’t see Drew move past her from the shock of a familiar face standing further away from her, but almost directly in her path. Instantly, a singe of heat tingled through Symone’s core; sending a volcanic blaze paralyzing her approach. Chills sprinkled across her arms, and the fine hairs on her neck stood on edge. Standing 6’4, adorned in a Brioni tuxedo that must have been custom made by the way it fit his broad shoulders and athletic chest, stood Mason Fuller, the FBI Agent that was assigned to their case.

His profile was daunting, slightly menacing, but charming at the same time. Symone was a master black belt, teaching martial arts during the day to adults and adolescents on a regular basis. Symone had never been afraid of anyone or anything in her life, but she was afraid of him. Not because of his career choice, but because of the unexplainable way her body reacted every time she came across his face.

"Symone, you stopped moving." Leah chirped in her ear. At the sound of her cousins' voice, Symone blinked and retreated.

"Fall back," Symone quipped. "Now." She turned to make sure Drew heard her. It was then she realized Drew was no longer standing next to her. Looking left, right then completing a twist in her heels, she searched for Drew, sighing heavily.

"Does anybody have eyes on Drew?"

Drew pulled up in front of a display, and her eyes sparkled.

"I'm in position," she uttered. "I can take it now."

"Drew, abort the mission!" Symone hissed through the earpiece.

"You don't understand," Drew protested.

"No, you don't understand!" Symone barked back.

"I'm so close," Drew said reaching her hand forward to grasp the item.

Six Months Earlier

Drew Patterson unrolled the large picture and laid it out on the kitchen table. “This is the Saliera.”

Drew’s eyes roamed from her sister, Brooklyn Patterson to their friends Leah Hunter and Symone Ellis. They stood around the table looking at the next item on their salvage list. Because it was a museum piece, the group agreed to let Drew take the lead since she was a curator of a local museum. Her knowledge of this precious item was essential to their operation.

“It looks heavy,” Leah noted.

“It’s a ten-inch gold figurine by Benvenuto Cellini, a sixteenth-century artist. It’s a little weighty but not so much that it would be a problem lifting,” Drew countered.

Leah peered closer. “But what is it exactly?”

“Plainly put, it’s a salt shaker. The man holds the salt, the woman the pepper,” Drew explained.

“Seriously, we’re stealing a salt shaker?” Leah responded.

“The appraised value is over fifty million dollars,” Drew stated matter of factly.

There was a steely silence that fell in the room as each one of them took in the weight of what stealing such an item could cost them personally.

"It's located in Vienna Austria. It'll be a good time to put to use all the years of foreign language classes we've taken," Drew said.

"But if we get caught..." Leah remarked.

Drew exhaled deeply. "Really Leah, must you start with the woe is me speech?"

Leah waved her off. "Whatever," Leah scoffed. "Whenever we do this, talking about the consequences should always be a part of the conversation."

"You weren't singing that same tune when Symone was the lead on the last job," Drew fused.

"Yes, I did, only you didn't hear it. Symone and I live together. Trust me, she heard it every day, until the day."

"Leah," Symone spoke. "The consequences are the same. We've been over this. We've fussed, fought, and cried it out. Did we not?" Leah didn't respond, and Symone continued. "We all came to the same conclusion. It's worth the risk. Everything is at stake here."

Brooklyn turned to her sister placing a hand on her shoulder giving it a slight rub in an effort to calm her. Drew met her eyes. "We're doing it," Brooklyn confirmed. "For the next six months leading up to the date, we meet every day to go over details, plans, and positions. Everyone remember your posts! We can't step out of place; the slightest slip up could mean the end for us."

Brooklyn unzipped her bag and pulled out a photo placing it in the center of the table on top of the picture of the Saliera.

"This is FBI Agent Mason Fuller."

She pulled out another photo and sat it next to his picture.

"This is his partner, Agent Brittany Stinson. They are currently looking for us. They don't know we're women, nor do they know how many of us there are. But they are good at their jobs and have always caught their man." She let the words sink in.

"Well that's refreshing," Leah asked. "How do you know all this?"

"I have a source on the inside."

Drew's eyes bugged out. "This source knows who we are?"

Brooklyn shook her head. "Don't be ridiculous! I would never give that information out to anyone. Just know, I've got my ways of getting information." Brooklyn cast a glance at Symone. "You're awfully quiet."

All eyes turned to Symone. Her dark brown eyes were stuck on the photos in the middle of the table. She reached behind her head and gave her neck a light squeeze. She'd run into Mason Fuller on more than one occasion now; once during their initial bank heist where she'd pretended to be an innocent citizen trying to make a deposit, and again, as she sat alone at Starbucks during her weekly sugar binge. Everything Symone ate went to her hips. Knowing this, she'd made it her business to watch her sugar intake. But once a week, Symone allowed herself the guilty pleasure to indulge. Seeing him the second time ruffled her feathers. Besides the fact Agent Fuller was searching for her hidden identity, she was attracted to him in the most sinful way, and it terrified her. Symone's eyes snapped up to Brooklyn.

"I'm fine."

"You don't look fine," Brooklyn said squinting at her. "Is there something you need us to know?"

Symone glanced from one person to the next. "No."

Brooklyn didn't believe her, but she'd get to the bottom of it later.

"Listen, ladies, our routine is the same as always. When we first set foot in the Kunsthistorisches Museum, we're only there to check things out. So, stay low key and don't bring any attention to yourself.

Present Day

An alarm was triggered before Symone could get to Drew.

"Shit!" She barked through the earpiece. The doors to the museum closed and security marched into place like a military force.

"Symone, do you have her?" Brooklyn questioned.

"No, I don't," she whispered sharply.

More security poured into the museum. Sporadic gasps and murmurs from onlookers crowded the space.

"We're locked in," Leah muttered. "Brooklyn, did you fix the camera system?"

"Of course," Brooklyn answered.

"I've got eyes on Drew," Leah stated.

"Where," Brooklyn asked a bit frantic.

"Left side, by the table of hors d'oeuvres."

They all glanced to her position. Drew gave a small smile and winked.

"I'm going to kill her," Symone growled.

"Hold your position ladies. We've got to get out of this in one piece."

"We have to abort this mission," Symone insisted. "It's not the right time."

"Why not," Drew casually interjected.

"You don't get to ask questions. You know we've been looking for you. Why haven't you been answering us?" Symone was livid.

"Calm down," Brooklyn ordered.

"Calm down? I'd like all of you to turn your attention to the right side of the room, black tux, golden brown skin, dark gray eyes, low haircut, looking like a god wrapped in flesh!" She spat the words out in one deep breath. A server passed her and Symone snatched a flute of champagne off the tray, tossing it back in one gulp.

"Damn girl! Sounds like you've got a crush," Drew taunted.

"What are you talking about?" Symone screeched.

"Um, you just described him using the word god. Do you need any more explanation than that?" Drew queried.

"I'll tell you what you should be explaining!"

"Ladies, you have got to calm down. We've come too far to get caught up now. Drew what did you take?" Brooklyn asked, always the reasonable one.

"I didn't take anything."

"So why did the alarm go off?" Leah questioned.

"I don't know. I guess we're about to find out."

The team of security marched through the crowd before a tall, thin man with bifocals pulled a microphone to his lips speaking in German.

"Ladies and gentleman, it seems there's been a false alarm. I assure you, this has never happened before, but all appears to be in place now. I apologize for the misunderstanding. If you would like to leave, the doors are open, but I would encourage you all to stay. Don't forget, tomorrow we're honoring Peter Paul Rubens, and I'd like it very much if you all would attend. Thank you for your patience. Please carry on."

"Carry on, the man says," Drew snarked.

"We're leaving one after the other. Now!" Symone barked.

Symone was the first to march out of the door. Other patrons straggled behind her unable to stay after the unease of the night's events. One by one, the ladies left in separate vehicles, making it their business to appear as if they didn't know each other.

Back at the hotel, they went about the business of packing their belongings. Drew was the last to enter and all heads whipped towards her.

"What," Drew asked innocently.

Symone pursed her lips, resting her hands on her hips.

“Okay, I know, I screwed up. You’re all right. I should’ve responded, but you have to understand. I’ve studied the Saliera for what seems like a lifetime. To stand in front of it, in all of its glory caused me to go blank for a moment.”

The women glared at her.

“I’m sorry,” Drew offered.

“Pack your bags, we’re leaving,” Symone quipped.

Drew huffed, mumbling under her breath. The ladies packed, checked out, and caught the next flight back to the states. As par the course, each sat separately in the airport, on the plane, and took different taxis upon leaving. It took them ten hours when they finally reached New York City.

“Let’s meet up at our place,” Brooklyn said. “We need to regroup.”

They hailed a taxi, instructing the driver to The Shops at Columbus Circle Mall. Once there, Leah paid the taxi, and they jumped into Symone’s Jeep Grand Cherokee. The car ride was quiet; everyone inside their own heads. Twenty minutes later they pulled into Brooklyn and Drew’s circular driveway and entered the house.

“Maybe we could do this tomorrow.” Symone stated. “We’ve already lost the opportunity to snatch the Saliera, so what’s the rush?”

"We need to talk about what happened," Brooklyn said. Leah grabbed the remote control and flipped through the channels.

"I'll tell you what happened. Little Miss, 'you guys never listen to meeee,' over here almost blew everything!" Symone yelled.

"I didn't almost blow anything. You're exaggerating as usual!" Drew shot back.

"Ladies!" Leah spoke up. They all turned to Leah then followed her eyes to see what had caught her attention. A CNN spokesperson was talking about a robbery at Kunsthistorisches Museum, in Vienna Austria.

"Turn it up!" Brooklyn said, as the women crowded the television.

"The false alarm turned out not to be false after all, as a hologram of the Saliera was left in place of the sixteenth-century artifact. The cameras seemed to be out of commission at the time of the heist, so no known suspects have been listed. This story is still developing..."

The trio turned towards Drew. A bright, sneaky smile lit up her face. In her hand, the Saliera sat in pristine state. Their mouths dropped.

"I told you, you guys should listen to me more often."

Chapter Two

He saw her, only her, in all her divine glory. The rest of the room, the art, the people, faded into nothingness. All he could see was her. She was beautifully breathtaking in her designer gown, and he appreciated every inch of her statuesque profile. He kept her in his periphery, moving in such a way to remain just out of her line of vision. A smile creased his lips as she moved so effortlessly through the exhibit. She never stopped to notice the men in the room stopping to admire her. Something else had her full attention.

The blare of the alarm caught him daydreaming. Agent Mason Fuller was snatched back into the present. Images that had been unclear, quickly came into focus as the angst in the crowd grew. He momentarily lost sight of her. Mason found himself still searching as his ear piece hummed to life.

"Fuller, you got eyes on the mark?"

His partner, Agent Brittany Stinson was on the other side of the museum. She had been watching

Symone Ellis, too. But in all the chaos from the alarm, she lost her in the crowd.

"Fuller, Fuller, come in?"

Stinson scanned the crowd searching for their suspect.

"No eyes on this end," Mason finally answered.

"Checking the rear," Stinson answered; moving against the mass of people to see if she could spot Ellis.

Mason's eyes were peeled. He scanned the crowd in hopes of seeing the target of their investigation. But there was a part of him that hoped he wouldn't see her. That was his dilemma, his quandary. He wanted Symone Ellis for all the wrong reasons.

Symone sat down solidly on the couch. She was absolutely flabbergasted. There were a plethora of emotions she felt all at the same time, but her only physical reaction was to sit with her mouth agape.

"Say it ain't so," Brooklyn exclaimed. Her eyes were wide and bright. She smiled at Drew who sheepishly smiled back at her.

"Can I hold it," Brooklyn asked grinning from ear to ear.

"Yeah," Drew replied laughing.

"Are you sure? Can I? Please, can I hold it?" Brooklyn asked, playfully rubbing her hands together.

"Here girl," Drew answered. She knew Brooklyn was clowning her, but that was cool. She knew that was Brooklyn's way of letting her know she was proud of what Drew had done. And that's what she wanted to do, make her big sister proud.

Brooklyn sat down next to her kid sister. Drew handed Brooklyn the precious artifact. Immediately, Brooklyn appreciated the weight of it, but immediately after that, the absolute beauty of the Saliera overwhelmed her.

Leah was transfixed. She hadn't moved from her spot since seeing the prize in Drew's hands. This was the big score. Everything the group did, everything they risked was all for this moment. Leah's hands still covered her mouth. Symone broke the spell.

"Drew, I don't even know what to say," she began. All eyes were on Symone.

"There's a part of me that wants to scream and celebrate and shout 'cause you did it, girl. You lifted the Saliera!"

Drew smiled, accepting the compliment. Symone paused before continuing.

"But, there's another part of me that wants to cuss your ass out!"

"Wait, Wh-," Drew began, sitting up straight on the couch.

"We almost got caught, Drew. You almost got us busted! All the planning and preparation and studying for you to go off and freelance? Did you even see Mason? Did you even know he was there?"

Symone was beside herself. She flopped back on the couch and folded her arms across her ample bosom. The spell Leah had been in was finally broken. She walked the short distance from where she was standing and sat down next to Symone. She placed a gentle hand on Symone's leg. Leah was the empath in the group; always trying to hold everyone together. These three ladies meant the world to her, and she never wanted any kind of dissension to come between them. Leah was slow to state her opinion, but on this one, she kind of agreed with Symone.

Brooklyn leaned over to her sister and cupped one hand over her mouth as she loudly whispered in Drew's ear.

"...she called him Mason... Did you hear that?"

Everyone in the room heard it, and that was exactly Brooklyn's intention.

“Mason,” Drew mimicked singing his name like it was part of a hit song.

Drew snickered, and Leah smiled looking over at Symone.

Symone felt her cheeks getting hot but pushed her pouty lips out and re-crossed her arms over her chest with emphasis.

“That is so not the point, Brooklyn,” Symone shot back.

“Well, what is the point Symone,” Brooklyn fired back, standing to her feet. What was the goal? The goal was to steal the damn salt shaker, or pepper shaker or whatever the hell this fifty million dollar beauty is.”

Brooklyn looked down still holding the Saliera.

“We got the goods. That’s the only damn point that matters!” Her voice echoed through the house.

Leah dropped her head and Drew looked away. Symone glared at Brooklyn who stared back at her. The moment was heated, and the intensity nearly choked the oxygen out of the room.

“...and the fact that you called him Mason...” Brooklyn added, her previous silly smile returning.

Drew tried to hold in her laugh but couldn’t. She looked over at Symone who was still pouting like she did when they were kids.

“Come on Symone, we did it,” Drew added, trying to regain some level of composure. “Can’t you let that other stuff go and just enjoy the victory?"

"Straight up, Symone," Brooklyn chimed in. "We should be popping bottles and celebrating. But you'd rather harp on the shoulda, woulda, coulda's... pssst," Brooklyn replied popping her lips.

Drew got up from the couch and walked over to Brooklyn removing the salt shaker from her sister's hands.

"This... this solves all our problems... this right here," Drew continued, walking over to Symone and squatting down in front of her.

"This is what it's all about."

Drew took the salt shaker and placed it under Symone's exposed fingers making her touch it. As desperately as she wanted to, Symone couldn't resist wrapping her hand around the artifact and holding it. She unfolded her arms and examined the Saliera. It was magnificent and just as Drew suggested, the answer to all of their prayers. Still, Symone felt undermined. Drew would have never pulled a stunt like that if Brooklyn had been running the heist. The beauty of the Saliera began to fade as Symone held on to her hurt feelings. Roughly handing the treasure to Leah, Symone popped up from the couch and stormed out of the room. She was frustrated but outnumbered. She needed a minute.

Up until this point, Leah had only seen the treasure from a distance, but now she was holding it in her hands. Her eyes started to mist over as she thought about what this trinket truly meant. It was security; not just for the four of them but for everyone that mattered most.

A knock at the door broke the silence.

They each looked at each other.

"Are you expecting someone," Leah asked.

"No," Brooklyn replied looking concerned. There was another knock followed by several rings of the doorbell in quick succession.

"Drew?"

"No, I'm not expecting anybody. Who even knows we're back?"

Whoever was at the door wasn't letting up. Brooklyn had no choice but to answer it.

"Put that thing away," Drew said, waving at Leah. Leah didn't know what to do with it. She looked around for some place to put it. Symone heard the door and came from the powder room.

"...what the hell?" Symone gestured.

Brooklyn's heart beat hard in her chest. She looked back over her shoulder at the trio before peeking through the peephole. Breathing a huge sigh of relief, Brooklyn swung the door open.

"James!" Brooklyn exclaimed, reaching out her arms to the little man standing in front of her.

"Hey, Auntie Brook," James replied, hugging her tightly around the waist. Although they were of no blood relation, Brooklyn always looked at James like a nephew.

The remaining three breathed easier as well. Quickly, Leah stuck the salt shaker between the cushions of the couch.

Releasing her, James bounded into the family room where the rest of his aunts were.

"Hey Mom, hey Aunt Natalie," Brooklyn said, hugging her mom and then her aunt as they entered the home. Constance Patterson and Natalie Hunter had been friends since grade school. Their bond grew tighter throughout the years, with them having their kids around the same time. It's inevitably how Brooklyn and Drew grew such a tight-knit bond with Leah, Natalie's daughter, and Symone, Natalie's niece. Their friendship turned into a partnership when they decided to go into business together with Patterson Pharmaceutical.

"How did you all know we were home?" Brooklyn asked.

"I'm your mother, honey, I know everything," Constance said, sashaying in.

“And what Constance knows, I know,” Natalie replied, following in the sashaying style of her best friend and business partner.

Brooklyn closed the door behind the two and followed them into the great room.

“There’s my handsome fella,” Leah replied, opening her arms to James who ran straight into them. She hugged him tightly. Leah always missed him when they were apart. James was just what the group needed to shift the tension in the atmosphere.

Chapter Three

Agents Fuller and Stinson were still at the Kunsthistorisches Museum.

"Roll back the footage again," Agent Stinson said, speaking to the owner and security team.

"See here," she said pointing towards the screen. "The time stamp is going from five to eight pm. Three hours are missing. That's not a coincidence."

Agent Fuller was silent. He heard everything she said and Stinson was right, but he felt like they might be on the wrong track.

"Did you hear me?" When he didn't respond, Stinson snapped her fingers.

"Mason!"

That got his attention. Mason blinked, coming out of his trance and stared at her. Ever since their one night stand when he made the bad decision to sleep with Stinson, she'd been hinting at a relationship or 'exploring more of their attraction', as she called it. But while Brittany was attractive, Mason was not interested and tried to tell her gently that he wasn't looking for a relationship. But Stinson didn't seem to get it.

"Agent... Fuller," he corrected.

If she felt affronted by his accuracy, Agent Stinson didn't show it.

"I think it's time we bring her in for questioning," Stinson continued.

"I disagree."

"Why?" She settled her weight in her left leg crossing her arms over her chest.

"I don't think it's her. I need to make a phone call."

Fuller turned to leave but was halted by Stinson's hand grabbing his arm.

"What do you mean, you don't think it's her? We're on her trail because of your gut feeling. What's that you're constantly saying, always trust your gut? Now suddenly you don't think it's her? You've got to give me more than that, Agent... Fuller."

Stinson said his name with a little malice. Fuller sighed. "When the alarm went off, I had her in my sight and from what I could tell, she was alone."

"But you don't know that for sure."

"I was watching her. I think I'm pretty sure," Fuller rebuffed.

"But were you watching her surroundings?" Stinson continued.

He lifted an inquisitive brow at her. "Why wouldn't I?"

"I don't know, you tell me." Stinson stared him down, looking for the slightest hint of indecision.

Fuller chuckled. "You're serious?" His dark gray eyes hitched, bewildered at Stinson's passive accusation.

"I'm just making sure you're on top of your game, agent. Isn't that what partners are for?"

Fuller's smile was dry and tight, but he let it go. "You're right. Thanks."

Mason slapped Stinson on the shoulder and left the security room. He needed to clear his head. There was a bit of truth to her words, but that was for him to figure out. Not her. It had been a long night, so much so, that it was now eight o'clock the next morning. The investigation into the missing Saliera caused his boss to call all hands on deck. But it was imperative for Fuller to get some shut eye so he could think with a clearer head.

Back at his hotel, Mason drew the curtains closed and shed his suit, cuff links, and shoes. He sat on the edge of the bed pondering Symone's sudden disappearance. Was it possible he was crossing her off the list because he didn't want her to be a suspect? Or, was he going about the investigation all wrong? Mason thought about what he'd seen last night. There were a few times he spotted her with another woman, but they didn't stay in conversation. She'd only given the few people she spoke to minimal attention, most likely about the art, before moving on. He grabbed his cell phone and called the airport.

"Vienna International Airport," the woman answered in German.

Mason replied in her language, "This is Agent Mason Fuller. I'm investigating the missing Saliera at Kunsthistorisches Museum, and I need some information."

"What can I help you with, agent?"

"Has a Symone Ellis flown out through your terminal?"

There was shuffling, then several clicks through the phone as the lady entered in Symone's name.

"I'm not showing a Symone Ellis."

"Check again, please."

"Spell the name please, sir."

"First name, S, y, m, o, n, e, last name, E, l, l, i, s."

More clicks from her keyboard. "No sir, I'm sorry, but there's no name in our system that matches that one."

"Thank you."

Mason disconnected the call and stretched out on the bed. Maybe she was still in Vienna. He didn't want Symone to know she was a suspect because if she was indeed guilty, she would surely run. But the more he thought about it, Mason wondered if his investigation into Symone was more about proving she was innocent rather than guilty. With his hands behind his head, Mason murmured her name, "Symone... Symone... Symone..." falling off into a deep slumber.

Leah pulled her Infinity in front of Tompkins Square Middle School and parked.

"You don't have to walk me in, mom. I promise, it's okay."

"You're just saying that because you don't want your friends to see me kiss you on those cheeks." Leah pinched James' jaw.

"Moooom!" He moaned. Leah laughed and puckered her lips. James crossed his eyes and leaned in for her kiss.

"Muah!" she said laughing at the way he squirmed. "You've got your lunch?"

"Check!" he responded.

"And your homework?"

"Check!"

"And your cell phone?"

"Is only in case of emergencies, I know. Do we have to go over this every day?" James sulked.

"Yes we do, now quit slouching, or I'll walk you inside."

James looked horrified, causing Leah to fall into a heap of giggles.

"Oh come now, I'm not that bad."

"Mom please," he begged.

"Alright, go on now. I love you."

James opened the door. "I love you, too!"

He ran off, and she watched him from her car. Leah had gotten used to hearing her nephew call her mom. When her twin sister Nia, disappeared nearly eight years ago, Leah took James in, claiming him as her own. It had worked so well that she didn't have the heart to tell him she wasn't really his mother. Whenever it crossed her mind, Leah shook it off. The conversation was a heavy one. How do you explain to a child that their mother left for reasons unknown and never looked back? No, she couldn't. So, for now, things would stay the way they were.

Leah peered at the middle school. Previously, James had been a student at KIPP Charter School, but when hard times hit, she could no longer afford the tuition on her social worker salary. If she hadn't of purchased the Infinity outright, there's no doubt it would've been repossessed. When she could no longer see James, she pulled away from the curb.

"What is love? Baby don't hurt me, don't hurt me, no more."

Haddaway's 1993 hit song blared from her cell phone. Leah glanced down at the screen.

"Hey what's up?" She answered.

"We need to have a conversation," Symone said.

"I'm listening."

"Not over the phone. What time are you going in," Symone asked.

"It depends. How important is this conversation we need to have?"

"Meet me, Joey's Deli."

"I'm ten minutes from there. How long will it take you to get there," Leah inquired.

"I'm already here."

"Okay."

When Leah pulled up to Joey's Deli, she could see Symone sitting in a booth through the window. Leah slid her handbag on her arm and tightened the scarf around her neck bracing herself for the wintery breeze. The doorbell chimed when she entered; her boots click-clacked on the brick tile. When Leah pulled up next to Symone, she bent giving Symone a quick hug. Leah removed her sunglasses before sliding across from Symone.

"What I miss," Leah asked, adjusting in the booth seat.

"Breakfast, for one thing. You were gone before I had a chance to speak to you this morning."

"Sorry, I had some things on my mind, so I got an early start."

Symone gave a worried glance. She knew it was the anniversary of the day Nia disappeared, and every year Leah became withdrawn.

"That's a nice sweater. Is it new," Leah asked, wanting to take the obvious attention away from herself.

"It is actually," Symone replied, looking down at herself, admiring the newness.

"I love the drop on the neckline, but should you be buying new things with everything we're going through," Leah chastised.

"It was on sale, I couldn't resist." Symone tugged at the thick turtleneck sweater that hung in waves around her neck. "Anyway, are we going to ignore Mason Fuller's presence at our last job?" This time when Symone said it, there was no glint in her eye. Maybe the thrill was gone.

Leah frowned and squinted her eyes. "I don't think we should. I didn't want to bring it up last night after everything that was said. That's just one more thing we have to worry about."

Symone sighed. Last night after her Aunts Natalie and Constance stopped by, they'd been made aware that the family's debt was increasing. The pharmaceutical company their parents co-owned was taking major losses. Despite the fact they'd secured a fifty-million-dollar insurance policy last night with the Saliera, Leah's biological mother and Symone's adopted aunt, Natalie, informed them the property they inherited from their late grandparents was up for auction because of missed payments.

They'd all groaned. "How many payments have we missed and why haven't we gotten any notices?" Drew had asked.

Constance slid a glance at all of them, her brows furrowed. "We're not going to worry about it. This is one we'll have to let go."

"We can't do that! It's been in the family for generations!" Drew spoke up.

"Baby," Constance went to her and pulled her in for a hug. "We just can't afford it."

"How much," Symone had asked.

"Sweetheart," Aunt Natalie started.

"How much," Symone asked again.

Natalie closed her eyes. "With the debt from our business plus the amount of the property..." her eyes danced quickly across the room. “Seventy-five point four million dollars.”

Brooklyn fell into the couch, grabbing her chest as if the wind had been knocked out of her. Everyone went quiet, and Natalie and Constance tried to explain why it wasn’t a need to worry. Why it was best for them to let the property go.

“We’ve done all we could. We gave it a good run.”

But for Leah, Symone, Brooklyn and Drew, they knew what this meant. One more luxurious heist was in their future, if not more.

A brief silence fell over the table as Symone and Leah remembered the feeling of dread and anxiety after the conversation. A waitress approached their table, taking their order of coffee and tea.

“Brooklyn and Drew don’t seem interested in a conversation about Agent Fuller’s presence,” Leah said. “They’re satisfied enough that Drew lifted the salt shaker. And you know, if he was there, his partner wasn’t far away.”

Symone shook her head in agreement. “The only way they would be there is if they knew something was going down. What would give them that impression?”

Leah’s nerves were on edge. Up until now, the women had assumed they were low on the totem pole concerning the FBI. But the agent's attendance said otherwise.

"Maybe we should lay low for a while and find out what they know," Leah offered.

"Or maybe," Symone injected, "We should tell Brooklyn to check with her inside man about specifics. We need to know, what they know."

The waitress approached sitting down hot tea and coffee in front of Symone and Leah.

"Thank you," they both chimed.

"You're right," Leah said. "When should we bring it up?"

"Today. Whichever one of us see's Brooklyn first."

Chapter Four

“I don’t know how much more we can do here,” Agent Stinson said, moving the over easy eggs around on her plate. Although she was hungry, after not eating during the stake out at the museum, her breakfast was unappetizing. The best thing about this morning was seeing Mason first thing. Maybe it was the seasoning or lack thereof. Maybe she just missed home.

Agent Fuller hadn’t even bothered to order breakfast, instead settling on a cup of black coffee. Having a debriefing session this morning was Stinson’s idea, and Mason just wanted to get through it without confrontation or god forbid flirtation. Stinson easily blurred the lines between their professional partnership and her fantasies of more intimate moments to come. It was an on-going battle to keep her on track.

“I agree,” Mason began, pulling himself back into the conversation, “but until we talk with the chief of the German Federal Police, we have to stick it out.”

“That could be a problem,” Stinson replied, continuing to poke at her eggs.

“Why,” Mason asked. His forehead creased.

“I’m not sure they know we’re here.”

Mason sat his cup down hard on the table.

“How could they not know, Stinson?”

“I didn’t say they didn’t know, Mason,” she defended. “I’m just not sure they know we are here in an official capacity.”

Mason had left the responsibility of informing the GFP to Stinson. She said she would handle it.

“What the hell kind of capacity do they think we’re here on,” Mason rebuffed.

She hated it when he looked at her that way, such disdain, like she failed him again. Stinson was straight out of Quantico when she was partnered up with the infamous Mason Fuller. Everyone in the bureau knew Mason didn’t want a partner, definitely not a new partner, definitely not a female partner after what happened to his last one. But Stinson was full of herself after graduating at the top of her class. She determined she would prove the naysayers’ wrong who insisted she’d be better off working with someone else. Stinson did just what she said. She was Mason Fuller’s partner.

"I think something got lost in translation," Stinson defended. "That's all I'm saying, but I'm sure it won't be a problem."

Mason's temper was on a low boil, but it was quickly heating up. To undermine a foreign authority was not only against protocol, it could also make an already difficult situation worse. Mason downed the rest of his coffee in one gulp and got up from the table.

"Fix it," he commanded and walked off.

Stinson flopped back against the seat and slid the fork across her plate.

"After all that, it's still not enough..."

Brooklyn was frustrated, as were the other three. What Constance and Natalie shared with them shook the group to their very core. Sitting in Leah and Symone's living room, the girls contemplated their next move, if there was one. Although Leah and Symone talked about bringing up the 'Mason in Vienna' issue with Brooklyn, now didn't feel like the right time. The angst and anxiety amongst the girls was already at an all-time high. Symone decided that adding one more thing right now, was not the best idea. If Leah brought it up, of course the issue would have to be addressed, but Symone decided she would not initiate it.

"That's it, it's done," Leah said sitting on the sofa across from Drew. The room fell silent. Drew eyed Leah from across the room. Symone looked off into the distance, refusing to make eye contact with anyone.

"Whatchu mean it's done, Leah?"

Drew's voice was low but intense. The sarcasm was thick. Drew stared Leah down which heightened the tension in the room.

"You heard what Auntie Constance said, Drew. We are millions of dollars short even after all we went through; all the planning, the risks... Like Auntie said, we gave it our best shot." Leah threw her hands up, in a universal sign of surrender.

Brooklyn leaned against the wall. As Leah spoke, Brooklyn shifted her weight uncomfortably from one foot to the other. Drew didn't respond immediately. Instead, she dropped her head and steepled her fingers on her lap. When Drew did raise her head, she immediately glared at Leah. Her eyes were tight like it was difficult to see. Deep lines creased her brow.

"So, you giving up, huh?" Drew began. She didn't wait for Leah to reply. "I'm not surprised."

Symone was forced to return her full attention to the conversation.

"What does that mean, Drew?" Leah asked.

"Just what I said," Drew rebuffed. "I'm not surprised that you would be the one to throw in the towel, throw your hands up, walk away... Like I said, not surprised at all."

Now Leah was starting to get upset and re-engaged physically in the conversation; lifting herself forward on the couch.

Drew, that's not fair," Leah began pleading her case. "That's not fair at all. I have been here the whole time, doing my part. I have risked it all too, Drew, and I have a child to take care of, so I've been putting it all on the line not just for me but for him, too!"

Drew heard Leah but refused to listen.

"It's really not your fault, you know, that whole walking away thing," Drew smirked. "It's in your blood."

"What did you say?" Leah asked, scooting to the very edge of the couch. Symone's mouth fell open, and Brooklyn lifted herself from the wall.

"I said it's in... your... blood...," Drew clapped back, exaggerating every word. She scooted to the edge of her seat as well, and the two glared at each other as Drew spit out her next jab. "Ain't that what Nia did?"

“What the fuck did you say, Drew?” Leah jumped to her feet, and Symone jumped up with her.

“You heard what the fuck I said!”

Drew stood up, and Brooklyn cut across the floor. Drew started to close the distance between herself and Leah. Leah didn’t back down as she took a decisive step in Drew’s direction. The two were standing so close together their noses practically touched. This was Leah’s proving ground. Her fists were tightly clenched by her side. Leah was never afraid to take it to the street when she had to. And if that’s what Drew wanted, Leah was not about to play nice. Leah’s eyes grew tighter as she stared Drew down. One could easily see the muscles tightening along her jawline. Drew was the first to move. She’d stepped back to gain enough distance to swing. Foul words flew between the cousins; words you wouldn’t say to your worst enemy. Leah was cut deep. Drew’s words sliced enough to draw first blood. Leah didn’t hesitate to throw the first blow when Drew gave her the opening.

Chapter Five

"Leah!" Symone yelled chasing after her cousin. She reached out and grabbed her just as Leah pushed through the front door. The screen slammed in Symone's face. Symone rushed through and reached out for her again.

"Get off me, Symone," Leah yelled yanking forward.

"Can you just slow down for a second," Symone requested.

Leah whirled toward her, anger radiating from her spirit.

"We shouldn't leave like this."

"Well, I'll leave. You can stay. But that bitch was way out of line, and I'm not giving her a pass for that shit because she's the baby girl!" Leah fumed.

"I didn't ask you to give her a pass. I just asked that you not leave this way," Symone reasoned.

"How would you like for me to leave, Symone?" Leah insisted.

"If you could just breathe for a minute. Both of you need to calm down so we can resolve this."

Leah sucked her teeth. "There's nothing to resolve! You heard her. It's in my blood to give up and walk away!"

Leah shook her head. "I'm not staying around any longer than I have to."

Leah turned on her heels and opened the car door slamming it once inside. Symone watched her lips move as she continued to fuss to herself before pulling away from the curb. Her tires screeched on the asphalt, and Symone watched her hit the corner hard. A car horn blew in the distance; the driver no doubt yelling expletives at Leah.

Symone shut her eyes and blew out a deep breath. Inside the house, Brooklyn and Drew were in a spat of their own.

"Whatever, Brooklyn!" Drew said. "You're just going to let her hit me across my face and not do anything about it?"

"You deserved it," Symone said reentering the house.

Brooklyn and Drew both turned to look at her. Brooklyn's face fell when she noticed Leah's absence. "She's gone?" Brooklyn asked.

"Yeah and I think she took out a car on her way around the corner." Symone crossed her arms.

“I didn’t do anything but tell the truth,” Drew muttered. “And I’m not sorry.”

“You should be!” Brooklyn fired back.

“Oh, what is this gang up on Drew day?”

“No one’s ganging up on you,” Symone added. “And quit acting like Brooklyn’s supposed to take up for you every time you get yourself in a bind.”

“You were wrong,” Brooklyn said, “Dead wrong. Leah has no control over her sisters’ disappearance no more than I have control over the shit that comes out of your mouth, and you know it!”

Drew rolled her neck and twisted her lips. She knew her words were hurtful, but she was hurting, too.

“...shit...” Drew mumbled thinking about the words she said to Leah. Drew massaged her temples and then walked towards the door.

“Where are you going?” Brooklyn and Symone said in unison.

“To fix it.” Drew grabbed her keys and marched out the door. Symone sunk into the couch. “That girl,” she said.

"Get your asses back pronto, do you hear me? Why in the absolute hell would you not go through protocol?!"

Mason sat stone-faced as he listened to the Director of the FBI scream through the speaker phone. Slowly he took his gaze to Agent Stinson who stood ramrod straight in front of the bed, her lips so tight it would take a crowbar to reopen them. They were in Mason's hotel room. He was showering when she decided to knock on the door with their boss on the phone.

"Sir, I thought it was handled. Let me talk to him I'm sure we can resolve this," Mason suggested.

"It's too late! He doesn't want our help, and we have to drop the case."

Just when Mason didn't think Agent Stinson would speak up, she did.

"We can't just drop the case! We have a possible suspect!"

"You can and you will! It's your own fault. The only thing we can do now is hand over the information we've collected and leave it to them to solve on their own." The Director sighed. "I don't have time for this. These mishaps should never happen with agents like you two. Get back now!" The line disconnected.

Brittany didn't dare look over to Mason, but she could feel his glare from across the room. "Damn it," she yelled.

Mason moved, walking into the bathroom. She caught the back of him. Remnants of water still soaked his broad back and shoulders. A towel was thrown haphazardly around his waist. He slammed the door, and her head fell in her hands. Brittany was so busy trying to impress him, she skipped a slight detail in processing the papers that would inform the government they were pursuing a suspect in their country.

Brittany left Mason's room and went to her quarters to prepare her luggage. After an hour passed with no word from Mason, Brittany rolled her suitcase out of the door only to notice a cart sitting in front of his room.

"Excuse me."

The maid looked to her. "Has the occupant of that room checked out?"

"Danke," the maid responded, confirming what she already knew. Mason left without her. It seemed her day couldn't get any worse.

The pace of the treadmill increased as Leah punched an angry finger at the speed and incline buttons. When her feet hit the hardwood floors of her childhood home, she sprinted to the exercise equipment to blow off some steam. Drew's words ran cycles on repeat in her mind and running on the elliptical machine was all she could do to keep from going back to kick Drew's ass. Sweat dripped down Leah's face, and her braids swung from the messy ponytail she'd shoved them in.

The doorbell rang, catching her attention. Leah didn't want any company. She didn't want Symone trying to talk her into calming down, and she didn't want a pep talk. The doorbell rang again. Leah glanced at the clock on the wall. It wasn't time for James to be out of school and he wouldn't think to look for her there so she would just ignore it.

Unfortunately for Leah, someone was just as persistent at getting her attention as she was at disregarding it. Leah hopped off the machine and took steps to the stereo system. When the music rang out, she amplified the volume so it would drown out whoever was outside. Back on the treadmill, Leah ran hard; her lips moving to the song on the radio. Forcing her thoughts to a pleasant place, a childhood memory invaded her mind.

"Momma, can we make the flowers again like we did yesterday?"

"Did you ask your sister if she wanted to help us?"

"Nia, Nia, Nia!" Leah ran into their bedroom. Nia sat with her legs folded on the bed sulking; tears stained her cheeks.

"Don't cry Nia."

Leah went to the bed, throwing her small arms around her twin sister.

"Momma said we can make the flowers like we did yesterday." Leah knew Nia's favorite thing to do was plant flowers in their mother's garden. This perked Nia up.

"Grover didn't go far he'll be back," Leah said trying to convince her sister that their dog Grover didn't leave forever. "Come on."

She guided Nia off the bed, and although Nia was older by two minutes, Leah still took on the role as big sister most of the time. Leah took pride in being responsible for Nia. They played and planted flowers in the garden and the next day Grover did return.

Being able to help Nia was one of the best memories of her childhood. Leah couldn't understand why Nia wouldn't confide in her before her disappearance. Didn't Nia know Leah would've done anything to help her? Leah was lost in her feelings going from one question to the next.

"You know, you really should move this thing."

Leah snapped from her thoughts and jumped off the treadmill retrieving a handgun that sat on the dresser. With swiftness, she turned towards the voice squaring off with the intruder.

Drew held her hands in the air, a spare key dangling from her hand. "Don't shoot, Leah!"

Leah grabbed her chest and heaved a heavy breath. She marched to the stereo and turned down the volume. "What are you doing? I could've killed you!"

"I need to talk to you, and you wouldn't answer your door."

"That means go away! How did you know I was here anyway?"

"Because...," Drew glanced around the room. "This is where you go when you're missing her."

Leah scowled. "What do you want, Drew?"

Leah placed the safety back on her gun and sat it down on the table. Taking quick steps across the room, Leah snatched the spare key she kept hidden under a flower pot on her front porch from Drew's hand.

"What do you want?" Leah asked again crossing her arms.

"I didn't come to fight."

"You must have, or else you wouldn't be here." Leah's glare held strong.

"I'm sorry." It was Drew's turn to fold her arms. "I was wrong. I shouldn't have said those things."

Leah offered her no response.

Drew's arms fell. "I know it's no excuse, but when Nia left, it didn't only impact you it impacted me, too." She shifted her weight from one foot to the other. "I guess deep down, I've been watching and waiting for you to throw in the towel, too. I have this recurring dream that I'll wake up, and you'll be gone. It bothers me that no one knows where she is or what happened to her. How could Nia leave without leaving a clue, even to you, her twin sister? It's bugged me every day, and you're the closest thing to her I can blame." Drew's' eyes faltered. "I'm sorry. I haven't been a very good friend."

Leah visibly softened, turning her back against the wall to lean on it for support. Leah's eyes shut tight as she thought about Drew's words. It never occurred to Leah that everyone could've taken Nia's disappearance just as hard as she did. They all treated her like she would break at any moment. Making sure she was okay, checking on her daily, taking care of her responsibilities while she mourned her sister's disappearance. It had almost taken therapy to bring Leah out of her funk. That was eight years ago, and time had not made things easier.

Drew stepped in front of Leah reaching out to pull her into her arms. “Forgive me.”

Leah threw her arms around Drew. “Forgiven,” Leah replied, pulling her best friend in tighter.

“I promise to do better,” Drew offered.

“I’ll hold you to that.”

“Now that you love me again, you know we have to get this money.”

The air grew thick around them. Leah sighed, “Yes, I know.”

Chapter Six

Mason sat slumped in the fake leather connected chairs in the terminal of the German airport. Having his ass handed to him first thing in the morning because of a mistake Brittany made did not sit well with him. More than that, because of her sloppiness, they could very well lose the lead on the case; his case, the case that introduced him to Symone Ellis. Fuller prided himself on having a 92% closure rate. That was unprecedented for an FBI agent with his years of service. Mason even managed to keep an excellent close record after having lost a partner and being assigned a rookie partner straight out of Quantico. But soon, none of that would matter. One of the most high profile, career building cases was at risk of being snatched from him.

"Passenger flight 549 from Austria to Manhattan, New York will be boarding in fifteen minutes."

To hear the announcement over the intercom was a great relief to Mason. He was ready to get back home, but he knew there were consequences he had to face. As Mason stood in line waiting to board the plane, he contemplated how he would handle things with the Director. He had to stay on the Ellis case. He hoped the Director's threat was just an idle one, but the Director was not a man who made empty threats or false promises. Mason knew he had his work cut out for him.

Brittany wanted to be pissed at Mason for leaving her. *I'm his partner dammit*, she thought to herself as she exited the cab and headed into the airport terminal. But even as she cursed Mason for failing to be a good partner, Brittany knew deep down that it was her error that caused the rift between them, and the ass chewing they got for it. The terminal was crowded, and Brittany wasn't as well versed in German as Mason was. She leaned on him during the trip for translating and pretty much leading her where she needed to go. Brittany became frustrated trying to navigate her way through the foreign airport, having to stop every hundred feet to ask someone if she was headed in the right direction. Most of the people she ran into were not English speaking so that pissed Brittany off even more.

By the time she got to the gate, the flight had already boarded, and the stewardess was closing the door to the tarmac.

"Please wait!" Brittany yelled as she was forced to run to try and catch her flight. Brittany wasn't sure the stewardess even understood what she said so she yelled again and ran even faster to get to the door; her bags falling off her shoulders as she went.

"Please, please...," She thought quickly of the German word Mason used, "Bitte!" She remembered as she neared her destination. The stewardess finally turned in Brittany's direction. At last, Brittany stood in front of the stewardess waving her boarding pass wildly so the stewardess could see it. The stewardess shook her head as if it was too late, but Brittany was insistent.

"I have to get on that plane," she demanded. "Bitte, Bitte," she begged. The stewardess went to the desk, and Brittany assumed she was calling the plane to see if they could board her. When the stewardess took the pass and opened the door to the tarmac, Brittany was incredibly relieved.

"Danke! Danke!"

Brittany didn't wait for the door to fully open before she pushed passed it and headed down the tarmac at a near jog. She didn't want to spend another moment in Austria especially with her and Mason on the outs. By the time she reached the entrance to the plane, she was already looking for him. He may have been on another flight, she didn't know, but her instinct was to look for her partner, even though she was sure, Mason had no interest in seeing her right now. The on plane stewardess wasn't willing to allow Brittany to wander down the aisle in hopes of looking for her partner. The plane waited for Brittany, and she needed to get seated immediately so the plane could take off. Brittany had no choice but to go to the seat she was being ushered to.

Mason was settled in his seat and waiting for the signal that the plane was ready to taxi down the runway. But they seemed to be delayed at the gate. Any kind of setback didn't help his disposition. And then he saw Brittany. Mason saw her looking around like she was looking for him. Instinctively, Mason dropped his head, hoping that she didn't see him. It might have been petty, but Mason was not in the mood to deal with her right now. Mason didn't look up and was relieved when the stewardess indicated the plane was preparing for takeoff. He would much rather sit next to a stranger than his partner right now. That's how much she had pissed him off. That's how disappointed he was with Brittany.

As the plane finally began to proceed down the runway, Mason finally relaxed in his seat. He leaned back on the headrest and closed his eyes. His thoughts were immediately of Symone, and not

Symone the criminal, but Symone the woman he desperately wanted to get to know.

"So did y'all kiss and makeup," Symone teased as Leah and Drew came through the door where they'd left Symone and Brooklyn. They had to figure out what their next move would be.

"Yeah, after she tried to shoot me," Drew replied smirking in Leah's direction.

"What the hell?" Brooklyn asked, eying both of them; Leah first and then Drew.

"She snuck up on me! Scared the shit out of me," Leah exclaimed, defending herself.

"I told y'all she didn't need that gun," Symone chimed in, shaking her head.

"Gone mess around and shoot somebody for real."

"Well, everybody can't be a black belt fashionista like you," Drew teased. "Hiyaaa! In six-inch Jimmy Choo's and shit!"

Drew stood up throwing a high kick into the air. Everybody fell out laughing as she imitated Symone's signature attack stance. Symone popped her lips and rolled her eyes at Drew and the other two for laughing with her. But it was funny, and

Symone joined in as Drew continued to show off her lack of skills.

As the laughter died down, Brooklyn, beginning to look pensive, changed the subject.

"Alright ladies, for real, what are we going to do about this money?"

The jubilant mood in the room quickly shifted, taking on a much more serious note. Drew joined Brooklyn at the dining room table. Symone and Leah followed. The group was quiet for a while, contemplating what they could do to bridge the gap between what they had and what the family still needed.

"How much do we need again," Leah asked trying to do the math in her head.

"A whole hell of a lot," Drew remarked placing her head in her upturned hands.

"Given the value of the salt shaker," Symone began, "and considering we need enough to not only cover the back taxes and bail out the business but provide a cushion while the company tries to bounce back..."

"And something for our damn trouble," Brooklyn added.

Symone cut her eyes at her friend.

"When did we decide that Brook," Symone asked, folding her arms across her buxom chest and sitting back in the chair.

"That's an understood, Symone," Brooklyn shot back.

"When did it become an understood?"

"When we decided to put it all on the line for the family, that's when," Brooklyn asserted without wavering.

"Brooklyn does have a point, Symone," Drew added. "Think about it. I mean we are all doing all right, but being a museum curator? It's for the love of the art baby, not the money. And I know you love teaching your martial arts students and all, but what happened last year when class enrollment dropped off that semester?" Drew didn't wait for Symone to respond. "Things got tight, and you were scrambling for a minute."

"They did Drew, but I bounced back," Symone quipped. She shifted uncomfortably in the seat as Drew continued.

"Brooklyn's doing fine, Brook is always fine, but having a little extra for a rainy day I'm sure wouldn't hurt, would it Brooklyn?"

"Naw, sis, it sure wouldn't," Brooklyn agreed. Symone expected allegiance between Brooklyn and Drew, and the upturn of her lips demonstrated how she felt.

"And I mean no disrespect, but you know social workers don't make no money. And Leah ain't in it for the money. But she's got James to take care of.

Having some extra money now and something for when baby boy gets ready to go to college or whatever? Come on Symone. If we doing this thing, we need to get our ends, too."

Leah nodded her head in agreement. It would make things much easier with a safety net. Although she hated to admit it, Symone knew they were right. It took her a minute, and Symone made them wait while she contemplated. But she saw the look in their eyes. Symone knew that if they were not all united on the plan, what they so desperately wanted to accomplish wouldn't happen. There was a time to be practical, and there was a time to make sure that not only did the people she cared most about survive, but thrive.

"As long as we don't get greedy," Symone began.

"We stole a multimillion dollar salt shaker, Symone, and it still ain't enough," Brooklyn reminded her. "We need to get paid!"

Drew and Leah chimed in. "for real," "that's right, Brooklyn!"

"Okay, okay, but we have to be smart about this. We have to plan, review, work all the angles and plan for every contingency."

"Come on Symone," Drew interjected. "We are professionals."

"Sho' you right!" She and Leah slapped a high five.

"I got your professionals," Symone quipped.

"So what's our target?" Brooklyn's question turned the conversation serious. The ladies grew silent, each thinking about what would be the next best move. They had a significant deficit to breach.

"The problem with stealing merchandise is getting rid of it," Leah asserted. "Dealing with all the back channels, covering our tracks so it can't be linked back to us..."

"Paying the damn middle man," Drew added, "that cuts into the profit margin."

The ladies had a point, and as Symone thought about it, she paced back and forth.

"So where are we with the salt shaker?" Brooklyn inquired. "Before we move on to the next, we have to make sure we have some traction on liquidating that very expensive asset." She continued. "We can at least put a stop gap on the back taxes and shore up the company until the next score."

"Don't you think it's a little soon to try to move it," Symone asked.

"Especially since your little heartthrob was there," Leah chimed in.

"Let's not start," Symone shot back.

"Brooklyn, was Agent Mason Fuller there?" Leah teased.

“Yes, he was,” Brooklyn said, nodding her head affirmatively.

“And did she or did she not reference him as a god, Drew?” Leah continued the tease.

“That she did,” Drew readily agreed.

Symone was embarrassed. “Y'all play too much,” she countered; her cheeks flushing. “But I agree with Brooklyn. We need to get some traction on moving the Saliera while we figure out our next move.”

“I’ll put the call in,” Drew said.

“Remember to use the burner,” Brooklyn reminded. Drew rolled her eyes.

“Thanks for the reminder, sis,” Drew whined. She hated it when Brooklyn treated her like a child.

“Why don’t we do a bank for the next one,” Leah offered. “With cash money, we can turn it over quicker, no middle man, less hassle.”

“That all sounds good,” Brooklyn began. “But you do remember what happened the first time we tried to do a bank?”

She did, and so did the rest of the group.

Chapter Seven

"Step forward, left leg first. Remember your hands, Carl."

Symone approached the young man and grabbed his fist.

"If you remember your legs and not your hands you won't be able to hold your position. Remember your hands." She stepped to his side and demonstrated. "Feet, step, legs, hands."

"Okay." He said.

"You got it, come on together, let's go."

They stepped completing the technique without error.

"Again!" Symone said.

Their steps continued to align as they practiced over and over.

"Good job!" She patted him on his shoulder and glanced at the clock on the wall. "Tomorrow we'll be working a little later than usual since you all will be fighting one another. Don't try to show out and just remember your steps and focus. You'll do fine."

The young men gathered their bags and filed out of the room one behind the other. Symone made her way to the shower room. Inside, she attempted to clear her thoughts but failed.

Symone didn't want to feel stressed out, but sometimes she couldn't help it. Her family's pharmaceutical business was thriving in the beginning. They'd all been surprised when the corporate income flourished into the multi-millions, but that wasn't without bank loans they'd needed to get it off the ground. The family was confident they would never want for anything. But, three years ago, all that changed. Not only had the business taken a hard loss, but they all went nearly bankrupt trying to keep it afloat; investing their own monies into the sinking ship. When they began to receive late payment notices from the property they inherited from their late ancestors, their parents were certain it was over. Now the millions they needed to keep the business going had landed on the four of them. And even though her aunt and uncle knew nothing of their thievery, it still felt like a ton of bricks. If they didn't get the money, the bank would collect what was owed, and the business would be shut down. Thoughts of the impending heist floated around Symone's head as she showered, dried, dressed and left the facility in route to her favorite place.

Now inside Starbucks, the smell of roasted coffee and the buzz of keys being tapped by local writers, sitting in their secluded spaces, filled the room. In line, Symone shifted the scarf around her neck. She smiled when the woman in front of her stepped aside, and she came face to face with the cashier.

"Hey Symone, will you have your usual today?"

"I think I'll go for a power lunch, the string cheese, fruit tray, bag of popcorn and bottled water."

"Fabulous."

The cashier typed her order in. "Eight dollars."

Instinctively, Symone pulled out her Visa and handed it to the lady. Happily, the cashier swiped the card, but it declined. The cashier frowned. "Um, its saying insufficient funds."

This time Symone frowned. "Try it again."

The cashier slid the card through again, but the machine beeped indicating that the Visa was no good. Thoughts of Drew's words were brought to the forefront of Symone's mind.

"I know you love teaching your martial arts students and all, but what happened last year when class enrollment dropped off that semester? Things got tight, and you were scrambling for a minute."

Symone lied when she said she bounced back. She hadn't; instead, she robbed Peter to pay Paul; going between two loan establishments to make ends meet. That was a confession Symone wasn't willing to make.

"It's on me."

A baritone voice beat behind her. Symone stiffened turning slowly to face him. Agent Mason Fuller stood so close to her she could smell his cologne.

Suddenly, her mouth was dry, and she needed that water faster than ever.

Mason's tongue traveled across his bottom lip; his mouth parted into a dazzling smile. For longer than necessary, they held each other in sight; hyper-aware of the connection that drove them both insane. Mason reached passed her handing his MasterCard to the cashier, which she happily took.

"No!" Symone said snapping out of her daze. "I've got cash." She fumbled for her wallet.

"It's okay, really, I don't mind," Mason said, covering her shaky hand with his. His movement pulled him even closer and a spark of energy coursed through their loins.

The cashier swiped the card before any more protesting could be done. Her line was getting long, and she was trying to make employee of the month.

"Should I add anything to this order," the cashier added.

"I'll take the Cafe Mocha," Mason answered.

"Mmmm those are good, I might have one for lunch," the eccentric waitress beamed.

"Tell me about it," he said setting his sights on Symone. "They have just the right amount of whip cream to share with someone special."

Symone tugged at her scarf. The material felt like a blanket of heat on her skin.

"Thank you," she said. "You really shouldn't have."

His eyes traveled the length of her, landing on all of her curvaceous assets. "I don't mind... really. Do you care to sit with me for a moment?"

"I'd be remiss to say no, don't you think?"

A devilish smile crept across Mason's face. "You have no duty to me. I'm not that kind of guy. However, I would hope you'd take pity and allow me a moment of your time."

Who was Symone kidding? Right about now she wanted to sit in his lap. She pursed her lips. "Sure, why not?"

"That's what I'm saying."

They chuckled and found a seat next to the window. He produced two straws that she hadn't noticed he'd taken before.

"One for you, one for me." Symone noticed that the straws had no protective covering.

Symone shook her head adamantly, "I couldn't."

"Of course you can, I don't have cooties."

Symone threw her head back and laughed. Her laughter was music to his ears.

"That's a beautiful laugh you have there, Symone."

Her smile slowly fell at the mention of her name. She cleared her throat.

"Thanks."

Mason sipped from his Cafe Mocha. "So, what is it that you do for a living?"

Symone crossed her legs under the table and sat back.

"I'm a martial arts instructor."

His brows lifted in surprise. "Now, you're just getting more interesting by the second."

"I'm surprised you don't already know it."

"Why would you say that?"

"You seem to be stalking me. First the bank, then at Starbucks, now here you are again, at Starbucks," she decided to leave out the overseas trip. That little tidbit would be too much information, and she wasn't certain that he'd known she was there. "I've been coming here for years, and I've never seen you until a few weeks ago."

It was Mason's turn to sit back in his chair. When he first saw her at New York Bank and Trust, she was standing in line waiting for a teller. Mason wasn't one to ogle a woman, but seeing her from the back tingled his spine. Unable to pull his eyes away from her, Mason got details of her side profile when she turned to look up, then swept a watchful eye around the establishment. Mason thought she'd missed him, but she did a double take and they were caught in one another's gaze. Mason obviously made her uncomfortable because she fidgeted with her fingers before returning her attention in front of her. The bank was robbed behind the scenes that day. No rush of criminals with masks covering their faces, guns drawn, screaming at the top of their lungs. No. This robbery was committed by professionals who slipped behind the scenes without masks, speaking like billionaires with business to handle at the bank. It was only when the alarm sounded that Mason even had a clue something went down.

Symone pretended to be a concerned spectator, and he went straight to her to protect her in the event things got crazy. But the thugs he waited to show their faces never did. After reviewing bank footage, he noticed women; a handful of them dressed impeccably, never lifted their faces high enough to be captured on camera. Except for Symone. She was exposed, and she was his only lead. Mason's gut told him Symone was a part of the coup. But the flutter in his chest made Mason hope she was just an innocent bystander. The women entered but never exited, and that was what ultimately gave them away. Mason questioned Symone's reasons for being there under the guise of polite conversation.

"I'm going to stick around and see if I can help with anything, do you mind giving me your name and phone number should the authorities have more questions?"

"Not at all," Symone responded rambling off the information. When Mason asked for her address, she declined.

"If they need anything else, tell them to contact me."

It would've sent up another red flag, so Mason pretended to be a bystander as well. Now sitting across from her, Mason wished he could shed the agent inside and let loose his inhibitions.

"Well I don't know," Mason began. "You haven't done anything worth being stalked, have you?"

They were playing now. If this was her martial arts class, this would be the moment when they sized each other up.

"I'm not sure what you mean by that, but if I've been a good girl or a bad girl you still shouldn't be stalking me. What are you a detective," Symone asked, feigning ignorance. She didn't wait for his reply.

"Just know, I'm not afraid of you. I can kick your ass."

Mason couldn't help himself. It started with a smile, then a hearty laugh. His arm crossed his abdomen as his laughter picked up. Symone was smiling now. "Oh you find me funny?"

"Damn girl," he said putting his hands in the air. "I'm not a stalker, I promise."

"That's what a stalker's supposed to say."

His smile never wavered.

"I'm not a stalker. If we keep running into each other, it's for one or two reasons."

"Which are..." Symone started.

"You've been a very bad girl and I'm here to take you in, or we're destined to be together, and I'm here to take you in." Mason let that last bit linger in the air as his words wrapped around her like a warm blanket.

Symone sat up and reached across the table pulling his Cafe Mocha to her mouth. Mason watched her cherry blossom lips settle over the sweet treat as her tongue slid out to taste the whip cream topping. Her eyes never left him. A moan cruised through her vocals.

His eyes darkened, and he bit back a curse. Symone was feeling spicy, and it had nothing to do with the coffee and everything to do with him. Mason's phone rang cutting through their moment. He took it out without taking his eyes off Symone and answered.

"Fuller."

"We need to talk." Brittany's voice was an annoyance he didn't want to hear. It made Mason wish he'd checked his caller ID first.

"Later," he said.

"No now, it's important."

His sigh was disgruntled and dramatic. "Speak on it," he barked, losing patience. Mason had no intention of leaving Symone at the moment, so it had better be good.

"We're still on the case. I talked to the Director. We can't pursue the robbery in Austria, but we can continue the case we've built here in the states. I'm leaving the office now; do you want me to meet you at your place or mine?"

"Your place, thirty minutes." He disconnected the call.

Symone arched her eyebrows. "Hot date?"

"Not even close."

"Mmhmm."

"I have no reason to lie to you, Miss Ellis."

"No, you wouldn't would you. Mason, I've got to say, your memory is pristine. Especially seeing we've only had introductions once. After that fiasco at the bank."

"I'm an FBI Agent. It's my job to remember."

"Wow," Symone feigned surprise. "An FBI Agent."

Mason smirked. "It seems your memory isn't so bad either. You remembered my name as well."

She tilted her head in response. "You're not easy to forget," Symone mumbled.

He checked his watch. "I'd love to stay and chat, but something's come up. Can I take you to dinner tonight, Symone?"

An inner voice yelled at her, 'say no, say no'. "Depends on where we're going."

His smile was seductive and disarming. "It's a surprise but if you say no, I can't promise not to stalk you until you say yes."

Symone knew she had no business going out with Mason. Hell, she had no business sitting with him now, but she couldn't help herself. Wanting him had become second nature for Symone, and she needed to explore it.

Reaching in her handbag, Symone pulled out an ink pen. She grabbed his hand turning it over to his palm and wrote her number across the middle. “Tomorrow night,” she said, thinking about their plans to get rid of the merchandise they’d recently acquired. The day was still young, and Drew had a man who was willing to be their go-to person for the black-market transaction.

“Tomorrow night it is.” He wouldn’t remind her that he’d still had her number from the moment she gave it to him at the bank.

Mason stood and took her hand planting a heated kiss to her skin.

“Until we meet again.” He said. Mason didn’t wait for a response, leaving just as quickly as he’d manifested.

Chapter Eight

Drew tapped her nails on the bench as she waited for Symone to show. They were meeting to talk about Drew's connect, but Drew's mind was elsewhere. She had already checked the clock on her phone at least three times, and that seemed to just make the time go by even slower. It goes without saying, Drew was not long on patience. It was never her strong suit. But anytime Drew had downtime, a moment for her mind to wander, her thoughts always landed Drew in the same place, thinking about the same one.

Unlike her sister Brooklyn, Drew didn't have a magnanimous personality. She was much more of an introvert, and because of that, she had been shy in initiating conversation with the opposite sex. This man tempted Drew to break out of her proverbial shell and make the first move. Clearly, he wouldn't. Drew smiled as she thought about her mystery man. She considered him a mystery because even after all this time, nearly a year since she first noticed him noticing her, they hadn't had a single conversation.

He was a frequent visitor to the museum. Every time there was a new exhibit, Drew knew he would be one of the first in for the viewing. As Drew continued to wait for Symone who seemed to always be running late, she thought about the last time, 'he' came in. Drew was especially excited for the new exhibit, featuring Jean-Michel Basquiat, renowned New York Neo-Expressionist painter most known for his collaborative work with Andy Warhol. Basquiat was first recognized because of his raw, primitive style that drew national attention because of the graffiti he created under the pseudonym SAMO in the 1970's.

Basquiat was one of Drew's favorite painters. She worked hard to secure the exhibit and was ecstatic that she landed the deal. Although she was supposed to be working, Drew found herself standing in front of her favorite painting, "Red Leg King", 1981. Basquiat captured racial conflict and religion in human form against a backdrop of brilliant colors with his signature graffiti-esque play with shadow and light. The painting in 2012 sold for an estimated $14.5 million dollars to a New York City resident willing to display the piece in Drew's museum. Drew stood in front of the painting; totally encapsulated by its rawness and message. She didn't even notice him standing next to her at first; each lost in their own appreciation of the piece. It was only when he took a step forward did she pick him up in her periphery. Then Drew's focus changed. She was no longer enraptured by the art standing before her but the man standing close to her.

He was taller than her by at least a foot. His caramel skin played nicely against the crisp white t-shirt he wore. His shoulder length dreadlocks were pulled back just enough for Drew to see his strong jawline and neatly groomed beard. Drew's eyes dropped, and she noted how well his jeans fit; loose in all the right places, accentuating his slim waist against his broad chest. When she checked his footwear, he had on timbs. Nice, Drew thought to herself. A homeboy with an appreciation for art. She chuckled a little, and that's when he turned to face her.

Drew smiled as she remembered that pleasant moment of embarrassment. She had covered her mouth trying to stave off her smile, but he smiled in return. His eyes were soft, and his smile was brilliant. Drew caught sight of the deep dimples in his cheeks and smiled again.

"Mmhmm," Symone said, clearing her throat. "Who got you cheesing like that?"

Drew was summoned back from her daydream to the present.

"You're late," she quipped.

"But I'm here now," Symone replied, sitting down next to her on the bench.

"Where's mine," Drew inquired, noticing the single iced drink in Symone's hand.

"Oh, um," Symone sputtered. She knew she forgot something. She smiled, remembering the reason why. Drew noticed the change in Symone's face.

"Who got you smiling like that, while you checking for me," she teased. "Tuh, I already know."

Busted, Symone leaned over and pushed Drew shoulder to shoulder.

"Whateva," Symone shot back. Where are we with the broker?"

"I mean, he sounds alright, legit," Drew began. "It's hard to vet somebody like that without showing too much of your own hand, though."

"Yeah, that's the problem when you have to deal with somebody new."

"I don't like the fact that we don't have a whole lot of choice. Trying to move the Saliera ourselves is out of the question."

"I know," Symone agreed. "So what's our move?"

"Give me a few days to see if I can do a little investigating on this new cat, see if he checks out," Drew answered.

"Be careful with that," Symone cautioned.

"Always..."

Mason finished off the last of his coffee before exiting the car at Brittany's spot. The dread he felt walking up to the front door didn't even require words. She must have spotted him getting out of the car because she opened the door before he had a chance to knock.

Brittany was smiling. How inappropriate, Mason thought to himself as he crossed her threshold. He didn't bother to greet her. They had already done that on the phone when she interrupted his most pleasant encounter of the day.

"That's great news, right," Brittany beamed as she ushered Mason into her quaint living room. Mason flopped down on the pastel floral couch, barely paying attention to what she said.

"I'm glad you think so," he replied.

Brittany could see he didn't want to be there. After all the begging and prostrating she had done to get them back on the case, and this is the thanks she got?

"You ungrateful man," she grumbled, sitting down on the loveseat across from him.

Now she had his attention.

"Ungrateful? What?"

Mason readjusted himself on the couch; scooting up, balancing himself on the edge. With his elbows on his knees and his hands folded in front of him, Mason addressed her. Mason did his best to keep it cool, but what she said pissed him off.

"What the fuck do you mean?" Mason didn't yell, but his words were heated.

"Just what I said, Mason, damn," Brittany snapped back.

"You think me ungrateful because of what? You fucked up the case, now you cleaned your own shit up and I ain't kissing your ass about it?"

"I know I messed up, but I fixed it! The least you could be is thankful," Brittany replied. Frustrated, Brittany sat further back on the couch and folded her arms across her chest. She couldn't even look at him, she was so agitated.

"...you're delusional..." Mason scoffed.

"I might be," Brittany answered. Uncrossing her arms, she leaned forward leveling her eyes to meet his. "But at least I got my priorities straight."

Even though he knew the answer, Mason still raised the question.

"And I don't?"

"Hell naw you don't," Brittany snapped. "If you focused on the job instead of her ass, you wouldn't have lost her in Austria," Brittany continued. "That sounds like fucked up priorities to me Agent Fuller."

"So is that what you called me over here for, to throw that shit up in my face or was there another reason?"

Mason sat back on the sofa, spread both his arms to rest on the back of the sofa and opened his legs. Just as expected, Brittany's mouth closed and her eyes landed right on his crotch. He watched Brittany as her posture changed, and she leaned forward even more, damn near salivating. When she looked up, lips pursed, eyes sultry, Mason responded.

"Right..."

Mason got up from the couch and looked over his shoulder at Brittany before leaving. She watched him until the door slammed behind him. She only had one word to say.

"Damn!"

It was just before 6:00 p.m. She knew if she wasn't back to the shelter in time, they wouldn't let her in. Other women at the shelter already looked at her sideways because she was one of the only ones allowed in the shelter who didn't have children. They thought she was receiving preferential treatment. How do you get special treatment in a homeless shelter?

Nia covered her stomach with her fingerless-gloved hand as if that would stop the growling from being heard by others. Hunger was a friend she'd grown to know all too well since she left home. The line in front of her and behind her was long; longer than she remembered from the night before. She hoped they would still have room for her.

"Hey watch it," someone yelled from behind her. There was pushing and shoving, and Nia was momentarily caught in the chaos; being bumped by one person and then another. She didn't fuss. Instead, she put up her hand to block the next person from falling into her. Nia couldn't be mad at them. They were struggling like she was. They were all just looking for a safe place to lay their heads.

Chapter Nine

Brooklyn crossed her long legs, getting comfortable in her seat. Her arms rested leisurely on the wingback chair that sat adjacent from the large mahogany desk inside the office of Atlantic Bank of New York. Dressed in a black feminine pants suit and stylish white blouse, Brooklyn held her smile as she watched Brandon McGee speak to someone over the phone. Her leg bounced softly; her red fingernails tapping lightly against the chair. Today she was Jessica Daniels, a business consultant looking to secure a family keepsake in the bank.

"If you need anything else, give me a callback or shoot me an email." Mr. McGee shook his head up and down, "Yes, that will be fine. Thank you."

Mr. McGee sat the phone back in its cradle and looked to Brooklyn. "I apologize, Ms. Daniels, it seems nothing can be done around here without me." His face lit up with a smile. "Now, where were we?"

"You were giving me information about your safety deposit boxes," she said.

"Ah, yes." He placed his elbows on the desk and enclosed his fingers.

"Our safety deposit boxes come in different sizes, the smallest being a two by five and twelve inches long. Is there a specific size you're looking for?"

"The smallest size will do. I only need to keep an ancestral document inside. Let me ask you, would this document need to be insured or will the bank take care of that for me?"

"Unfortunately, the FDIC only insures funds that are in your account, but the box itself is kept in our vault. I would consider it safe, but getting insurance is always a good thing."

"I see."

"Do you have an account with us, Ms. Daniels?"

"No, I don't. I'm new to the area, so I'm looking to change institutions soon enough, which is why I'm here today."

"I understand. If you don't mind me asking, are you from the south? I couldn't help but notice your accent."

Taken back by the question, Brooklyn thought a bit longer than necessary on an answer. "I was born in Louisiana." She lied. "But I've lived in DC most of my life. Now I'm looking to settle here in New York."

"A bit of a traveler I see."

"Well when I was young I didn't have much of a choice since it was my parents doing, but now I've been presented with an opportunity of a lifetime, so moving is only fitting."

Brooklyn had lied before, but after recovering from the shock of his question, the lies eased off her lips like butter. In reality, she was from Savannah, Georgia. After her grandparents passed, her mom Constance and father Grant Patterson whisked her and Drew to New York at the age of thirteen. It was amazing that folks could still hear her southern accent, and being questioned about it always surprised her.

Brooklyn didn't like being questioned. It was none of his business where she was from and with that thought, she flipped the queries back at him.

"How much is the fee on the box?"

"The smallest boxes are one hundred and forty-four dollars annually, but if you prefer it, we could bill you monthly. Would you like to see the room? I'll show you how you'll have access if you decide to purchase one with us today."

Brooklyn beamed. "Of course."

Mr. McGee rose from his chair and closed his suit jacket. He was a heavyset man, and the jacket wasn't big enough to accommodate his girth while he sat. He wobbled around the desk, "This way, please."

Brooklyn followed him closely, glancing at her watch. It laced her wrist seeming just as ordinary as any accessory, but a closer look would reveal its true nature. Brooklyn considered herself the nerd of the group. She was brilliant in science and mathematics. It wasn't often that she applied her genius, but sometimes it came in handy. Like with the watch she'd built; it was smart enough to pick up camera sensors as she strolled behind Mr. McGee. The watch collected information on the position of the red eye lasers that were hidden behind the tinted frame of the security cameras. The days of old fashioned casing of banks were over when it came to Brooklyn. The only thing she needed was to keep her head level so none of the security cams would pick up a schematic diagram of her face.

The two rounded a corner and pulled up to a large closed vault. Mr. McGee slid his keycard inside, and she watched as a variety of lights counted down from red to yellow, then finally green. There was a loud click and the door popped ajar. Mr. McGee pulled the heavy door, and they stepped into a metal box that held containers lined up and down against the walls of the room. In the middle sat three simple metal tables. Mr. McGee wobbled to a box already open and pulled it out of the wall placing it on the table.

"Here's an example of the box you would be renting."

"Hmmm," she said examining the box closely.

"Mr. McGee," a woman called out, standing on the other side of the vault entrance. He glanced up, momentarily giving Brooklyn time to slip another electronic gadget underneath the metal table.

"There's someone else who'd like to take a look at a safety deposit box. Do you mind if they come in now?"

On cue, Brooklyn's phone sang out, and she pulled it from her purse taking a look at the screen. "I'm sorry, I need to get this."

"No problem," Mr. McGee said.

Brooklyn brought the phone to her ear.

"Hello?" she listened intently then gasped. "Oh my God! I'm on my way right now!" she disconnected the call.

"I'm sorry, I have to run." Brooklyn sprinted to the door. "I'll be back tomorrow to finish what we started here."

"Oh, okay sure," Mr. McGee called after her.

Brooklyn fled the building through the banks rotating doors as if the devil was hot on her heels. It made for a dramatic exit as she fell into the midday shuffle of pedestrians on the downtown sidewalk. Her heels took her across the street, two blocks down from the institution. As she approached a mobile dog grooming truck, the doors slid open, and Leah held a hand out to her.

"Thanks," Brooklyn said, quickly stepping inside.

"You were so good. Have you ever thought about becoming an actress?"

Brooklyn snickered. "Maybe I'll try it once we're done getting our coins. How's the display?" Brooklyn leaned towards the three, twenty-inch flat screen monitors that sat in a row.

"As you can see, the picture quality is good."

Brooklyn nodded her head in agreement.

"Come here, Danger," Brooklyn said speaking to the chihuahua they'd taken as a prop for their cover. Danger came on command and sat down next to Brooklyn. Reaching onto the table in front of the monitors, Brooklyn grabbed a doggie trip and gave it to her four-legged friend.

"You know he's never going to want to go home if you keep feeding him like that," Leah said.

"Danger's practically at my house every day anyway. The neighbors don't mind. I always take him home. Right now, they think I'm out walking him."

Leah shook her head and smirked. "And why'd they name him, Danger? He's not about to hurt anybody."

Brooklyn laughed. “You’d have to ask his owners.” She studied the monitor. “Yes, this picture is really good,” Brooklyn stated.

“No sooner than you clamped the sensor to the table, the screens lit up.”

“Good, good,” Brooklyn repeated. They had eyes inside the bank. Now it was about twenty-four hours of surveillance until they figured out the institution's daily operations.

Brooklyn sat back and pulled the clear sticky makeshift covers from her fingertips.

“I still can’t believe you made those,” Leah said.

“Why not?”

“Because it’s the last thing I would’ve thought of.”

Brooklyn cracked a smile. “They work like magic. Can’t leave my fingerprints behind, can I?”

“No, ma’am.”

“Have you heard from Drew and Symone?”

“Yeah, but I only spoke to them briefly so I could keep my attention on you. Drew’s going to approach her contact.”

“When?”

“Supposedly tonight.”

“Will Symone be with her?”

“I didn’t ask. Why? Are you worried?”

Brooklyn sighed. "I'm always worried when it comes to Drew. She's so determined to prove something, it makes me paranoid."

"That's true, but we don't need to hold on to the Saliera any longer. I can call Symone and ask her to stay with Drew."

Brooklyn thought for a moment. It would be smart for Symone to have Drew's back, just in case. On the other hand, if Drew suspected Symone was around to babysit her, she'd cry foul and throw a tantrum and possibly blow the connect.

"No," Brooklyn said. "Let her handle it."

There was a sharp bang on the door. Leah and Brooklyn whipped to the first monitor.

"Shit, it's the police," Brooklyn announced.

Quickly, Brooklyn and Leah moved, pulling a silver door over the monitors. Leah grabbed dog grooming shampoo, scissors, and a blow dryer and sat it in front of the doors that encased the monitors.

Brooklyn whistled to Danger, and he jumped into her lap, his tongue hanging out. She looked back to Leah and Leah nodded. When Brooklyn opened the door, she put on the brightest smile she could muster.

"Good afternoon officer, how can I help you?"

The officer perused Brooklyn from head to toe and smiled at the chihuahua.

"Good afternoon, ma'am. I've got my K-9 back in the truck, and he could use a good grooming. How long will you be here today?"

"Oh, until the rush hour is over, then we'll head to Fifth Avenue."

Danger wriggled in Brooklyn's arms and growled at the man in front of him. Brooklyn held the dog firmly and stroked his coat to calm him.

The officer seemed to be stuck in his thoughts. "I'm sorry, what is your name," he asked.

Brooklyn's mouth went dry. "Jessica," she held her hand out for a shake, "Jessica Daniels."

"If you don't mind me saying, Jessica Daniels, you... are... beautiful." He glanced down to her ring finger. "Is that Mrs. or?"

"Oh my goodness, thank you, and that's Ms. Daniels." Brooklyn feigned flattery and Danger growled again. Leah kept her eyes peeled on the officer, still unsure as to whether or not they had a real problem.

The officer pulled out a business card and handed it to her.

"This has my personal cell on it. If it's okay with you, give me a call sometime. I'd love to get to know you."

Brooklyn puckered her lips and peered at him.

"Officer if you don't mind me asking, did you see me enter the grooming van?"

He smirked, "Guilty."

"So then there's really no K-9 waiting for you in the truck, is there?"

"No there is, but it seemed like the perfect excuse at the time."

She chuckled, "I'll think about it," Brooklyn smiled.

"That's all I'm asking." He lit her up with a charming smile. "I'll let you get back to it. It was nice to meet you, Ms. Daniels."

She tilted her head in response, and he walked away. Brooklyn shut the door and turned to Leah.

"What the hell?" Leah said with her hands on her hips.

"I don't know, but we're not sticking around to find out. Wait until Officer Bob pulls off, put this van in drive, and let's get out of here."

Chapter Ten

When he walked through the museum doors, the fine hairs on Drew's neck stood at attention. This was it; she was going to ask him out. Drew knew she had an important meet up with the man who could help them unload the Saliera but for the moment, connecting with the man she'd been daydreaming about was far more important. Drew didn't have a lot of time. She had to make her move and make it quick; while at the same time, not making herself look foolish.

He was doing his usual stand and stare at the art and looking absolutely delicious. Drew could feel her knees getting wobbly and the thump of her heart pulsating in her ears. *You can do this Drew,* she thought to herself. Smoothing down the deep lavender sheath she wore over slim black slacks, Drew advanced in his direction. She opened her mouth slightly and blew out slowly trying to achieve calm before speaking to him.

He noticed her coming. He always noticed her. She was part of the reason he continued to stop by the museum, in addition to the art, of course.

Drew walked up immediately behind him and stood slightly to his left. That way, she had one last chance to appreciate his exquisite face, just in case he summarily dismissed her and rejected her forthright advance. This wasn't something Drew did before. She was used to occasionally being pursued, not pursuing. But she was willing to make an exception for him.

He felt her and the energy that emitted from her person. He knew that energy as he'd felt it before. They stood there, in that moment, vibing without speaking. The thumping in Drew's ears increased, drowning out the traditional silence of the museum. Her body vibrated as if a heavy bass beat blasted through six-foot speakers. Maybe this wasn't the best time. Maybe she should just wait.

"I've been waiting for you..."

Initially, Drew didn't hear him, couldn't hear him because of the nervous energy and the pounding of her heart.

"I'm sorry?" Drew's response was hesitant and barely audible. But he heard her and turned to face her. When their eyes met, it was like in the movies. Everything in the background faded into nothingness. The only thing that existed were these two people suspended in space and time. Drew met his downward gaze, and she saw everything she ever wanted in his dark brown eyes. There was no need to smile in her direction. His brooding eyes said everything Drew wanted to hear. And instead of being more anxious, surprisingly enough, the noise in her ears quieted. Her heart rate regulated and took on a steady beat that caused any signs of anxiety, fear or nervousness to fade away.

He thought to repeat his earlier statement when she spoke.

"Drew..."

"I know..."

He smiled and she smiled again.

"I'm Legend..."

Symone did her best to stay out of sight, but that was proving increasingly difficult as the museum had few visitors. She knew if Drew saw her, Drew would automatically assume Symone had no confidence in her ability to discern whether the connection would be appropriate or not. The Saliera heist was a big deal; it was Drew's baby. She masterminded the entire thing, so it would be hard for Drew to believe they didn't trust her ability to finish the job. At the same time, Symone couldn't help wanting to be there to support Drew, whether she wanted it or not. Drew and Brooklyn were like family to Symone. They were family. But this was business. The weight of the family legacy rested on all their shoulders, but Symone felt that weight a little heavier than the other girls. At least that's how she felt.

There was a certain expectation that Drew, Leah, and Brooklyn would come to their parent's aid. They were direct heirs to the Patterson and Hunter legacy. They were committed to saving the pharmaceutical company and the family's land by blood. For Symone, her blood was distant, not direct lineage. But Auntie Natalie and Uncle Derrick treated Symone like she was their own. They never differentiated how they cared just because Symone was not their child. Symone felt a deep abiding obligation to make things better for them. Symone felt she owed them so much because of the way Natalie and Derrick loved her.

Symone looked down at her watch. Drew was supposed to be meeting with the connection in less than ten minutes and here she was gawking and gazing up in some boys' eyes. Symone was so tempted to cross the room and demand Drew to focus on the job. There was a time and a place for everything and this wasn't either of the two. Symone's foot patted rhythmically against the concrete floor, shattering the relative silence in the museum. Symone wasn't really mindful that she was doing it. It was an involuntary reaction to her lack of patience. When Symone heard her foot taps echoing back is when she stopped. She looked in Drew's direction to see if the sound reached her. Fortunately, Drew was still daydreaming, looking up in that guys' face. Symone decided to move closer to Drew. She didn't want to have to reveal her presence, but she would if it looked like Drew wouldn't make the meeting.

Symone's foot tapping may not have gotten Drew's attention, but it certainly got the attention of Agent Stinson. Brittany was there, clandestine, unbeknownst to her wayward partner. She knew Symone Ellis was the key to breaking the Austria case and Brittany was like a dog with a bone. She refused to let go. Brittany had been tracking Symone ever since Brittany unceremoniously returned from the Kunsthistorisches Museum situation. Brittany was incredibly frustrated behind Mason's latest stint; leading her on and discounting her value to him. After he left her apartment, Brittany pulled out her computer, determined to make headway on the Austria heist; not to benefit Mason's career, but her own. They had Symone Ellis' name from the bank robbery months earlier. Symone willingly gave it to Mason when he relentlessly flirted with her while the bank was being robbed.

Brittany was sexually frustrated. She hadn't had a good lay since Mason. And for him to tease her on the very same couch they last screwed aggravated her even more. When he relaxed on the couch and opened his legs, she thought Mason was inviting her back to him. Just maybe he was ready to rekindle some things. Brittany thought Mason missed her as much as she missed him. *Fuckin' bastard...* But instead of inviting her in, Mason walked out. Brittany was left alone with nothing to show for their little encounter other than moist panties.

"I need a drink," Brittany said aloud. She dragged herself into the kitchen. There was a bottle of Merlot resting on the counter. Wine would have made a perfect refreshment after a steamy session with Mason. That didn't happen. Brittany smacked her lips and pushed passed the wine. She reached for the bourbon instead. In the upper cabinet, Brittany found an eight-ounce glass and filled it nearly to the brim. Reaching into the cutlery drawer, she retrieved a pinstriped straw and stuck it in her drink. Making her way back to the couch, Brittany picked up her computer and clicked open the file she kept on Ms. Ellis. Mason didn't know anything about this file. He didn't deserve to know. He was so deluded with Symone's looks, Brittany felt he no longer saw Symone as the criminal she was. Symone Ellis was a bourgeois street thug. Brittany decided that if Mason didn't do anything to bring Symone to justice, she would.

Drawing her mind back to the situation at hand, Brittany kept an eye on Symone while trying to forget about Mason sexually frustrating her. If Brittany could connect the dots, link Symone to that crime and who knows how many others, their Director would certainly take notice. She could even take the lead position from Mason. *That would teach his ass*, Brittany thought as she kept a close eye on her primary suspect. Brittany took note of Symone's focus. Just like the bank heist, Symone stalked around unassumingly, but Agent Stinson knew there was more to it than that. Symone kept watching this couple. No matter where Ms. Ellis moved in the room, her eyes never left the pair. But they didn't even seem to know she was there.

Symone's incessant foot tapping was no mistake either. She was anxious about something, constantly checking her watch and staring at the twosome. Was that Symone's man, two-timing her with the beautiful girl he was standing with?

Brittany smiled at the thought of the perfect Ms. Ellis being cheated on. But the guy looked kind of young. Maybe Symone was a cougar, playing with another woman's cub. Is that why she was watching them so closely? The smirk on Agent Stinson's face widened at the thought.

Ms. Ellis' attention momentarily drifted away from the couple and she looked around the museum. Agent Stinson dropped her gaze, moving a few feet to the right. Brittany feigned interest in a sculpture immediately in front of her. Her cover would be blown if Symone saw her. After a few beats, Brittany looked up from down-turned eyes to see whether Symone spotted her. But Symone's attention had returned to the couple. Agent Stinson stepped from behind the sculpture and watched Symone watch them.

Maybe Symone was casing this museum for another heist? Maybe that's why she was here.

After turning in the dog grooming truck to the warehouse where they kept it, Leah and Brooklyn parted ways. It was almost time for James to get home from school and Leah wanted to be there when he arrived. Because of their stakeout, James rode the bus to school. She hated for him to come home to an empty house. Leah pulled her car into the driveway. After turning off the ignition and removing the keys, Leah grabbed her purse and exited the vehicle. She stopped at the mailbox before going inside. Typically, she would leave that task to James, but he forgot more times than he remembered.

Leah tucked the mail under her arm and closed the mailbox door. She made her way up the front walk and retrieved her keys from her purse. Once inside, Leah turned off the alarm, kicked off her shoes and put her purse on the entry way table. James was always hungry when he got home from school, so Leah made her way to the kitchen. Sitting the mail on the counter, Leah perused the refrigerator and then the cabinets to find a suitable snack for her growing boy. Deciding on fresh fruit, cheese, and crackers, Leah pulled the items from their respective places and sat them on the countertop next to the mail.

Leah paused for a moment, catching sight of the corner of one of the envelopes.

Hmmm... she muttered as she fished the envelope out. State of New York, she read on the return line. Leah double checked to make sure the letter was addressed to her. Sure enough, her name and address were listed behind the translucent paper midway down the envelope.

What does the state of New York want with me, Leah wondered as she tapped the short end of the envelope on the counter and tore open the other end. Leah's ears perked up as she heard the bus pull up outside. She contemplated putting the envelope aside to get James' snack prepared, but her curiosity was certainly piqued. Leah pulled the folded letter from the envelope and opened it. She scanned the top and part of the body, and then Leah began to read more intently.

Ms. Leah Hunter;

It has come to the department's attention that you are the acting guardian for James Hunter, son of Nia Hunter. However, in completing our due diligence regarding the aforementioned minor, we have determined that no official transfer of guardianship has taken place and as such, the minor is considered without a caregiver.

Leah's mouth fell open and her hand started to shake as she continued reading.

A court hearing has been scheduled for July 25, 2017, at which time the judge will determine the appropriate course of action for said minor. If you are interested in obtaining legal guardianship of said minor, please be prepared with the necessary documents to determine your appropriateness to be his lawful caregiver. The minor's parents will also have opportunity to establish their fitness as his birth parents.

Just then, the front door opened.

"Mom, I'm home..."

Chapter Eleven

Drew seemed flustered. Although Symone couldn't hear their conversation, she could see Drew blush from across the room. What the hell? Symone thought. Briefly, Symone cast a glance around the museum. She could count on one hand how many people floated around the building and there seemed to be fewer and fewer by the minute. Symone turned her attention back to Drew, but caught the woman in her peripheral that moved from corner to corner since Symone arrived. Dressed down in a baseball cap, blue jeans and a black shirt, the woman seemed oddly out of her element. But Symone couldn't be bothered with her presence because she was too focused on Drew.

Their conversation seemed light and Drew's body language went from casual to languid. Then they moved, Drew going one way and the man going another. Symone glanced down at her watch. Drew missed the opportunity to meet with her contact and Symone tried and failed to calm her own nerves. Giving this operation to Drew to headline was a bad idea. They should've known better. While Symone was silently chastising Drew, Drew returned to the hall and exited the building. Quickly, Symone went after her. Outside, Symone jumped in the driver seat of her Nissan Maxima and pulled out a few feet behind Drew.

They drove for what seemed like ten miles before Drew pulled into an empty parking lot of an abandoned warehouse. Symone glanced in the rearview mirror and pulled to the side of the road watching Drew from a distance. A Chevy Tahoe pulled into a spot next to Drew's car, and she exited with her handbag in tow. The tinted windows on the truck made it hard to see who Drew's contact was, but it put a flirtatious smile on Drew's face. Symone frowned. The girl was flirting with everyone today and Drew was not that type. Symone wondered who this man was and she would surely get the details when this was over.

Just as Symone thought it, the driver side door of the Tahoe opened and the handsome brother from the museum stepped out, trailing a path around the truck to open Drew's door and help her in.

"Is that her contact?" Symone said out loud.

Symone's mind raced and she glanced in her rearview again. It was then she noticed the Buick

Encore sitting idle at a green light a few feet back. Horns blew at the vehicle from impatient drivers wanting to get on with their day. The Buick made a left turn going out of Symone's sight. She took her focus back to Drew and the mystery man. They were pulling out of the parking lot and Drew was in his truck.

"This is just getting more interesting by the second," Symone spoke to herself. She grabbed her cell phone pondering a phone call to Brooklyn. But, she'd given Drew this much space so instead, she opened up the camera on her phone and took a snapshot of his license plate.

"Don't get any bright ideas, sucker."

Symone pulled off behind him, making sure to keep a reasonable distance. The street sat on a warehouse row with only a few cars coming along here and there. They made a left turn and Symone followed them. When another car turned behind her, she caught sight of the Buick pulling up to her rear. Creases outlined Symone's face as she frowned. Was this person lost? She wondered. Traffic slowed to a red light. Symone took another look at the Buick and saw the driver.

"Hell no..."

Her heart rate increased and she checked her side mirrors. Closing her eyes, Symone pulled in a deep breath. It was the woman in the ball cap and although her face was half concealed by the baseball cap, the features Symone could make out were oddly familiar with the picture of Agent Brittany Stinson, the FBI Agent assigned to their case.

"Shit! Shit! Shit!"

There were so many questions running through Symone's head. How did Stinson find them? How long had she been watching? Symone remembered her from the museum, but how long before that had she been watching? The light turned green and traffic moved.

Symone thought fast. If Agent Stinson was simply following her, then she'd led her to Drew and their contact. "Shit!" she spat. This was bad news. As the cars in front of her moved, Symone held still. She waited until the light turned yellow then sped forward. Surely enough, Agent Stinson hit the gas and was on her bumper. The light switched to red and Symone slammed on her brakes coming to a screeching halt. The Buick Encore rammed into the back of her Nissan causing Symone's seatbelt to lock, holding her in place. Smoke billowed from the hood of Agent Stinson's car. They were in the middle of the intersection and traffic was now completely at a standstill. Symone grabbed her cell phone and sent the picture of Drew's mystery man's tag to

Brooklyn's phone, then erased the message and the picture.

Symone looked toward the Tahoe catching Drew's eye. Twisted in her seat, Drew's eyes were as big as saucers; her hand resting lightly on the guy's shoulder. Busted, Symone thought. Symone knew she would get an earful later from Drew, especially after she explained herself. His truck came to a slow stop and Symone shook her head 'no'. Drew frowned and Symone mouthed, go. Drew turned back in her seat and spoke to her driver. He pulled along down the road. Symone watched them as they disappeared around the corner.

When Symone's phone rang, it didn't surprise her. She answered it without checking the screen while simultaneously exiting her Nissan.

"I'm fine, everything's okay but my car may be totaled."

"I'm sorry to hear that."

The timber of Mason's voice slithered through her eardrum like a whispered caress. Symone shuddered.

"Mason, my God, I thought you were someone else."

"Yeah, I'm sorry about that, too. Are you okay?"

"Um, yeah physically, for now anyway. It seems I've been rear-ended."

"Tell me where you are and I'll come to you."

A smile tugged at the corner of her lips.

"That's not necessary. I'm very capable of handling this on my own."

"I'm sure you are, but I'd still like to help. After all, you said your car might be totaled. You can't very well drive away in it."

He had a point. But something about being around both he and Agent Stinson at the same time didn't settle well with Symone. Agent Stinson approached her.

"Why would you slam on your brakes like that," she asked; her voice elevated.

"Excuse me? The light turned red and had you not been following me so closely this wouldn't have happened. I sure hope you have car insurance."

Brittany glanced around nervously then sighed. "Of course I do, this is a government vehicle."

"Too bad for you. I'm sure your boss won't appreciate you tearing up their property."

Symone held her hand out to receive Brittany's information.

"Property of the Federal Bureau of Investigations. Agent Brittany Stinson," she read aloud.

Mason barked through the phone. "What?"

"It looks like I've been hit by one of your colleagues."

Symone heard Mason let out a deep breath and a few expletives.

"Tell me where you are, now," he commanded with an ominous growl. It should've frightened Symone, but it didn't. The commandment sent a fire straight to her panties. Symone gave her location.

"I'm not far from you. I'll be there in five minutes."

Their line disconnected. A text message chimed and she opened it immediately.

Call me. It was from Brooklyn.

Symone sent back a text. Not now. Give me a minute.

Sirens could be heard from a distance.

"Did you call the police," Brittany asked; piercing Symone with an obnoxious glare.

"I haven't had time to call them, but I'm sure one of these lovely people stuck in traffic here made the call for us."

Symone rubbed the back of her neck.

Frustrated Brittany asked, "Were you wearing your seatbelt?"

"Fortunately for you."

Brittany snorted then snapped. "Whatever. You should take driving lessons. If I didn't know any better, I'd think you caused the accident on purpose."

A Crown Victoria pulled up and parked alongside them, along with three police cruisers. The officers got out and walked toward them. In his Crown Victoria, Mason shut off the engine and stepped out. His long strides brought him to Symone and Brittany quickly. At the manifestation of him, Brittany's jaw hung open. "What are you doing here," Brittany asked.

He grabbed Symone by her arm. "Are you okay?"

He saw annoyance in Symone's face. The same beautiful face he couldn't seem to get out of his mind.

"What's wrong?" His voice was thick and stern.

"How dare you blame me for your reckless driving," Symone said speaking to Brittany. "Why on God's green earth would I purposely cause this accident? More than that, how could I? I didn't make you run into the back of my car! If you hadn't been on my ass, this would've never happened. You know what..." Symone shifted her weight from one foot to the other. "I should sue you and the Federal Bureau of Investigations. I'm sure they wouldn't take it lightly being dragged into court." Symone rubbed the back of her neck again.

Mason glared at Brittany.

"Look, that's not necessary," Brittany said, looking from Symone to Mason. "I can pay for the damages out of pocket."

"What about my medical bills, can you pay for that out of pocket, too?"

Brittany held back an eye roll and sucked her teeth.

"Yes, I can pay your medical expenses."

Symone pursed her lips, determined to give Agent Brittany Stinson a hard time. "I don't know. I think we should have this on record."

An officer approached. "Tell me what happened."

Symone rattled off the details of their accident while making sure not to lay off pointing the finger at Agent Stinson.

"Do you need an ambulance, ma'am?"

Laying it on thick, Symone inhaled and exhaled. "No, I'll find my own way to the hospital."

"Please," Mason reached for her arm again. "Let me take you."

It took everything in Brittany to keep her smart comment to herself.

Symone's eyes traveled up and down his extended frame.

"Are you sure that's such a good idea?"

"It's not a problem at all."

Symone glanced back at Brittany. "Sure, I guess."

Mason walked her to his Crown Victoria just as a tow truck pulled up to holster Symone's car. The officer took down Brittany's information as she watched with scathing contempt her partner helping Symone into his car.

Mason re-entered the driver's seat and buckled his seat belt. He pulled away from the accident and Symone didn't miss the irritation on his face when his eyes roamed across Brittany's menacing glare.

What was up with these two? Symone wondered.

"I'm glad I called when I did," Mason spoke.

"Why were you calling?"

"To confirm our date tonight." He swept an eye over her. "Looks like we'll have to postpone it."

"Yeah, but look on the bright side, we still got a chance to be in each other's company."

He smirked, "It's not exactly what I had in mind. Hopefully, we have a chance to try again."

A smile pulled at her lips. "Of course."

Mason reached out and tucked a strand of hair behind Symone's ear. It was hard for him to keep his hands to himself but he was trying. The movement sent a ripple of warmth through Symone. She could not seriously entertain this man and she'd told herself this so many times. But here she was allowing him to take her to the hospital. And what would she do when it came time for him to take her home? With the kind of man, she knew him to be, Mason wouldn't simply drop her off at the E.R., and she couldn't very well take him home for more reasons than one.

Pulling out her cell phone, Symone sent a text to Brooklyn. *Meet me at New York Presbyterian Hospital in twenty minutes. I'll give you the details once we leave.*

Fifteen minutes later

There was a knock on the door. "Come in."

Mason peeked his head inside of the hospital room. "I wanted to check on you. What's the verdict?"

Symone smiled. "Why didn't you come back here with me?"

"If you decide to sue the department I don't think it would be in your best interest for me to hear your medical results since I'm a part of said department. That and it is your personal information."

He stood by the door with his hands in his jean pockets.

"Since when do you care about my best interests?"

The doctor re-entered the room.

"How are you?" The doctor said holding a hand out to Mason.

"I'm good, thanks for taking care of my girl."

"That's what I'm here for. Are you the husband of Mrs. Ellis?"

There was a gleam in Mason's eyes as he responded, "Not quite." Mason spoke to the doctor, but he watched Symone. If he didn't know any better, Mason could have sworn he saw her shiver.

"Here's your referral to see the chiropractor. You can make an appointment at your earliest convenience."

"Thank you," Symone responded. "Am I free to go?"

"Yes, ma'am. Take care of yourself."

The doctor left the room, but Mason and Symone continued to gaze at each other. Symone didn't miss him referencing her as his girl and she enjoyed the sentiment more than she should have. Mason's eyes took in her full lips, disheveled hair and dark brown eyes. He was moving before he realized it. Symone stood and Mason reached out;

his fingers clasping a fierce hand around the back of her head.

"You can slap me later, but I've wanted to do this since our first encounter."

His mouth fell to hers in a scorching kiss that lit a torch in her gut. Soft full lips meshed together as they sucked and pulled the plump folds of their mouths together. A moan rose up in Symone's throat meeting Mason's animalistic growl.

Someone cleared their throat. "Am I interrupting something?"

Symone pulled away flustered, turning to meet Brooklyn's surprised face.

"Brook!" Symone said. Symone's thoughts were jumbled. But Mason's piercing gaze was steady on Symone's succulent lips.

Slowly Symone turned back to Mason. "Um..." she rattled, "My friend is here to give me a ride home. I've taken up enough of your time today." Her voice was sultry with a throaty heaviness.

"I don't mind taking you home, Symone," he offered. "In fact, it would be my pleasure."

The heat rising from Symone turned into a furnace. Symone shook her head vehemently. "Raincheck," was all she said.

He pulled back from Symone, finally giving Brooklyn a glance. Then, Mason returned his eyes to Symone. “I’ll check on you in a little while,” he assured.

“Okay.”

“This isn’t over,” he promised. Mason’s eyes fell to her lips again before he walked away.

Mason gave a slight head nod to Brooklyn as his stride took him passed her and out of the room.

Brooklyn arched a brow. “Somebodies got some explaining to do…”

Chapter Twelve

"What was that all about?"

Drew returned her eyes to the man she was sitting next to. He could ask the question now that they were removed from the commotion.

Drew wasn't sure what she should say next. The level of shock she was experiencing from the situation with Symone following her, nearly paled in comparison to the man sitting next to her. Her heart was already in her throat when she entered the car to meet the connection. When she saw him, Drew's heart nearly stopped. But she had to compose herself, to some degree, and for more than one reason. Taking a deep breath, Drew faced her source.

"I'm still trippin'," she began. The same heat that rose in her cheeks when she stood in front of her dream man in the museum just minutes before, was the same exact heat she felt now.

"Did you know, I mean, did you make the connection?"

Legend smiled. She was an uncanny beauty, and her innocence made her even more attractive.

"No," Legend replied. "I had no idea you were you."

They both smiled. Even their open conversation sounded clandestine and mysterious.

"So...," Drew began, fidgeting in the passenger seat. "Does this change anything for you?"

Legend sat back, relaxing in the driver's seat. When Drew raised the question, she turned away from him, unsure of his response. This could be a precarious situation, and he understood not only the question but her hesitation.

"I come into the museum for two reasons, Drew," Legend began. "I love the artwork... the masterpieces hanging on the wall..." He reached across and gently touched her chin, turning her face toward him. "... and you..."

Drew felt her protective wall giving way under his penetrating gaze. Legends' eyes could melt wax, baby, and Drew found it hard to maintain her composure. She felt like he was looking through her, like he really saw her. She flashed to how the girls bashed Symone about her man crush and decided to shore things up. *Keep it tight Drew, keep it tight,* she chided herself before answering.

"So does that mean our arrangement is compromised," Drew inquired, trying to bring the conversation back to a professional level, even though her knees were weak.

"I can still move the merchandise, that's not a problem," Legend replied confidently. And then he smiled, slowly. "I'm a professional," he joked.

"Okay, Mr. Professional," Drew teased back.

Legend liked Drew's quick wit. He had designs on her and wanted to be clear. "The real question is," Legend began, "will our professional relationship keep us from having a personal one?"

Brooklyn didn't wait until they were out of the hospital before lighting into Symone.

"Explain!"

"Keep your voice down," Symone replied, looking around embarrassed.

"Damn that Symone," Brooklyn exploded. "Explain!"

Symone grabbed Brooklyn firmly by the wrist and wrestled to lead her the remaining feet to the exit door. Brooklyn resisted, not caring who overheard her.

"You gone tell me what the hell is going on, or I will turn this hospital all the way out. Now, explain!"

Brooklyn stopped their forward momentum just short of the door. Symone had no choice but to stop with her.

"Brooklyn," she began, looking over her shoulder to see just how much of a scene they'd already caused. "I will explain everything, promise. But can we please go outside with this, please?" Symone looked around again, and ducked her head in her shoulders when she caught the glaring eyes of onlookers.

Brooklyn reluctantly acquiesced, allowing herself to be dragged out of the door. But the automatic-action door hadn't completely closed before she addressed Symone again.

"What the fuck were you thinking? Don't answer that, 'cause clearly, you weren't thinking... well, not with your damn head anyway."

Brooklyn snatched away from Symone and walked several feet down the paved walkway. Symone chased behind her, all the while trying to figure out what she could say to Brooklyn. Symone could see from her slothful approach that Brooklyn wasn't having it. Brooklyn's hands were on her hips, and she was standing flat-footed, waiting.

"It's not what you think," Symone started as she got within ten feet of Brooklyn. It was the warm-up. Symone prayed there was more in the well.

"I didn't plan for it at all," Symone continued when there was no audible response from Brooklyn. "See what happened was, I was trailing Drew to her meet-up, and I realized, somebody was following me; the same person I saw in the museum when I was first watching Drew. Can you believe the trail rear-ended me? She was so busy trying to see what I was doing she wasn't paying attention to what she was doing and hit my doggone car!"

Symone rubbed her neck for effect. Brooklyn still didn't say anything; just shifted her weight from one foot to the other. The scowl on her face was unmoved.

They were standing face to face now; one looking pensive and hopeful, the other still pissed off. It was awkwardly tense. Symone looked away more than once, unable to bear Brooklyn's glare.

"None of the shit you said makes a bit of damn difference."

Brooklyn was seething at Symone's shortsightedness.

"But I was just—"

Brooklyn cut Symone off before she could finish. Symone's lame ass explanation was making things worse not better. Exacerbated by the whole situation, Brooklyn responded. Symone turned away knowing her excuses weren't working.

"He saw me, Symone... he saw me, with you..."

When Symone turned back around to face Brooklyn, her mouth was agape. The realization as to why Brooklyn was so pissed registered like an anchor dropping on dry land. Her hands immediately went to her head as flashes of their past crimes and the connections Mason could now make raced through Symone's mind. She knew she fucked up.

"...damn girl...I'm—"

Again, Brooklyn wasn't there for the excuses or the apologies.

"You jeopardized everything, everything Symone! And for what? Some FBI dick?"

Symone had no reasonable response, so she said nothing.

"... you make me sick..."

Before anything else could happen, before Symone could muster up any new words to try, Brooklyn popped her lips, turned and walked away. The sinking feeling Symone had in the pit of her stomach was nearly enough to make her physically ill. As judgmental as she had been for the side steps and perceived missteps of the other girls in the group were nothing compared to the catastrophic mistake she just made. Symone couldn't even convince herself that it was a matter of her not thinking. It was so much bigger than that. Brooklyn was right. She could have screwed the whole thing up because of a man.

Leah contemplated whether she should share the letter from the court with the girls. Everyone was already dealing with so much. This would be yet another thing to pile on the already highly stacked pile of anxiety driven things to worry about.

"Mom, did you hear me?"

James and Leah were having dinner, but Leah didn't have much of an appetite. She had been so lost in her own thoughts, she scarcely heard James talking.

"Sorry, big man," Leah replied; disengaging from her own worries and focusing on what was really important.

"I need you to help me decide what I'm going to do for the science fair this year."

"When is the fair again?"

"Mom, seriously?" James asked. "We have only been talking about it for the last two weeks. The date is even circled on the calendar on the refrigerator."

"Remind me again, James, please?" Leah said, smooshing his hair. She knew he hated that, but it would always bring a smile.

James got up from the kitchen table and walked the short distance to the refrigerator. Removing the brightly colored magnets that held the calendar in place, James returned to the table and placed it in front of his mom.

"See," he pointed to the date circled in red. "July 25th."

Leah looked down at the calendar and indeed, that date was circled in bright red marker. It was like a jab to the heart.

"I see," she replied without looking up. James repositioned himself at the kitchen table and resumed his dinner, shoving a forkful of green beans and mashed potatoes in his mouth. He didn't wait until he sufficiently chewed before addressing his mother again.

"So, think mom, what are we going to do?"

Leah knew James was talking about the project. But what was she going to do about him?

Brittany couldn't believe her partner left her stranded at the scene with no regard as to how she would get home. Even before the tow truck could arrive, her Captain was on the phone. Somehow he learned of the car accident before she had opportunity to tell him.

"I want a full fucking report on my desk immediately!"

"Yes sir," Brittany answered. "I have called for a tow, but I don't have a way back to the station." She started to rat her partner out; tell the captain how he'd left her stranded. But before she could decide whether that was the next best move, the captain responded.

"Agent Stinson." He waited until she replied to ensure she was listening.

"I know you are not trying to make that a concern for me, are you?"

Brittany knew better than to reply.

"I don't care if you take a bus, train, cab, walk, hitchhike or tie a string to a gottdamn carrier pigeon, you get your ass back to this office and get me my damn report!"

Chapter Thirteen

Drew paced back and forth. What the hell was Symone doing following her and why wasn't she answering her phone? Drew slid a hand across her forehead and paused, trying to settle her racing heart. What was going on? One minute she was having the most pleasant conversation with Legend and the next they were almost caught up in a traffic jam. Even after the exchange had been completed, Drew was stilled troubled by whatever was going on with Symone.

Legend had reassured Drew that knowing she was the seller wasn't a problem for him. So they'd proceeded with Legend transferring dividends from his buyer's account to Drew's offshore account and Drew in return handing over the Saliera. They parted, going their separate ways so Legend could hand over the buyer's prized possession and Drew could find out just what the hell was going on with Symone.

Just then her phone chirped. Swiftly, Drew connected the call.

"Hello!" irritation laced her voice.

"I can explain," Symone began.

Drew rested her free hand on her hip. "You were following me, that much is clear."

"Yes, I was, but it's not because I didn't have faith in your ability to get things done. It's because I didn't want you to be alone. I just wanted to have your back in case anything went down. I even took a snapshot of the guy's license plate."

"Bullshit!" Drew fumed.

"You were there to watch me because you didn't believe I could get the job done. Just face it Symone, you've always thought I was a screw-up."

"What the hell, Drew! I haven't always thought that at all."

"Lie to me again," Drew said. "I swear to God, Symone!"

Drew's feet moved, and she began to pace. "You could've ruined everything! I had the Saliera on me. What would've happened if I'd been caught up in that accident, huh? With a fucking federal agent no less!"

Drew was screaming; completely and utterly livid with Symone.

"I see you've talked to Brooklyn," Symone stated flatly.

"Sure have, and she told me everything I needed to know. You should pay more attention to yourself and the way you're fucking up with Mason," she spat, saying his voice in a singsong mock.

"You know what, you're right. From now on I'll mind my own business."

The line died, and Drew's eyes bugged out.

"Hello?" she screeched. "Oh I know that heifer didn't just hang up on me!"

Drew snatched the phone from her ear and glared at the screensaver floating around her phone. Symone had surely hung up. She had some nerve! Drew mused.

"I need a fucking drink."

Drew jumped in her car and drove to Lamar's Pub off Davison's and Bowery. Whipping the vehicle into a parking spot, Drew climbed out and stalked through the door. At first glance, the bar seemed infested with young adults. But a closer look revealed men in jerseys that supported the team they favored crowded around pool tables and flat screen TV's to watch the game.

Drew strutted to the bar flopping down on a barstool.

"What can I get you?" The tall, slim bartender questioned. The man eyed her closely already noticing that her day wasn't going too well by the frown broadcasted in her gloomy features.

"I'll have whatever you've got that's strong."

The bartender's brows rose. "That could be a number of things."

Drew let out a discontented breath. "Look, just make me something. Surprise me. Just give me what you've got."

The bartender slid away uninterested in getting into a tiff with her. When he returned, a short glass with two ice cubes and clear liquid was produced. Without hesitation, Drew knocked back the liquor. The piercing sting of the alcohol coursed down her throat settling in her belly, bringing an instant heat to her core. Drew sighed. It was just what she needed. A fast-paced melody shrilled from her smartphone. Drew cast an eye at the screen. It was Brooklyn, most likely calling to find out her whereabouts.

"After all," Drew mumbled, "I can't be left alone. I'm incapable of doing anything without assistance."

The ringing phone stopped but picked right back up with the same tone moments later. Drew rolled her eyes and answered, "What can I do for you, sis?"

"Where are you?"

"I'm at where I'm at, and I'll be where I'll be, is there anything else?"

Brooklyn was silent for a moment.

"I'm not your enemy," Brooklyn offered.

"What. Do. You. Want. Brooklyn?" Drew was passed the small talk. She whistled for the bartender. "Can I get another one, please?" Drew watched him make her drink.

"How about this, when will you be home?"

"I don't know."

Drew's nonchalant answers annoyed Brooklyn to no end. But, she understood her kid sister was probably still angry about everything that happened with Symone earlier, so she tried unsuccessfully to reach her another way.

Drew grabbed the glass from the bartender and rotated the barstool she sat in resting her back against the bar. Her eyes floated around the room stopping short on a familiar face sitting at a lone table watching her.

"I don't want to fight with you," Brooklyn assured her. "I just called to talk."

Approaching her now, Drew watched with inquisitive eyes as an incandescent need covered her.

"Sis, I gotta call you back."

Drew closed the call before Brooklyn had a chance to object. He was standing mere inches in front of her now. Drew tossed back the rest of the liquor allowing a quaint smile to pull at her lips.

"Hello again," she offered.

"Good evening, I couldn't help but notice you sitting here at the bar."

"Is that right?"

"It is."

"I guess next you'll tell me it was meant for us to see each other again?"

A deep groveling laugh oozed from him. "It doesn't seem that I need too, since, you already know it."

Drew took another glance around the room before settling her eyes back on him. "It's nice to see you outside of the museum. If I didn't know any better, I'd think you were following me." She paused, "Are you following me, Legend?"

He took a step towards her, closing the gap. "What if I told you I was, would you be alarmed?"

"Should I be?"

His tongue snaked out of his mouth and swiped at his top lip.

"Maybe..."

Drew's sour mood was removed and replaced by a courageous one. Legend's gaze fell to the now empty glass in her hand.

"I was getting ready to leave, would you like to join me?"

Drew inhaled a deep breath. "As a matter of fact, I would." She rose from her seat and placed the glass on the bar. In her small handbag, Drew fished out loose bills and dropped them on the counter. She turned to Legend.

"I'm ready whenever you are."

Legend held a hand out. "After you."

Drew sashayed out the door, going straight for his truck. Like a gentleman, Legend opened her door allowing Drew to get in before saddling his own seat behind the wheel.

Legend's cologne was alluring enough that Drew wanted to lean over and bite him. But at least for now, she would keep her mouth to herself. On the road, Legend glanced to her.

"I've never met a woman like you before," he admitted.

"And by a woman like me, you mean..."

"Beautiful, daring, professional, ambiguous."

Drew smirked. They pulled to a red light and Legend cast a glimpse out the driver side window catching the attention of a woman sitting in a nearby vehicle. A smile rested on his face and he winked before pulling off.

"I get the feeling we could build a powerful partnership, Drew."

"I'm sure we could always be of some assistance." Her voice was low and throaty; her mind flirting with the alcohol that rested in her system.

Legend drove a few miles before entering what Drew thought upon first glance was a gated community. Giving a second look, their destination revealed a mansion style home enclosed on its own land.

Drew looked around. “This is all you?”

A suave smile graced his face. “Would you like the grand tour?”

Drew’s sight fluttered to the tall windows, broad grassy lawn, and pink blooming flowers that decorated his entryway. Legend cut the engine.

“Those flowers are called Naked Lady.”

Drew almost laughed. “How apropos,” she said.

“Why is that? Do you plan to become my naked lady?”

Drew squirmed in her seat. She reached for the door handle letting it fly open. The breeze coated her heated skin and she welcomed it. They climbed out and approached the flowers. Drew bent to smell them.

“Careful,” Legend halted her descent. She studied him questionably. “They’re beautiful, but that lovely smell contains a poison that can cause cardiovascular collapse.”

Drew straightened instantly. “Why would you plant these flowers?”

"The same reasons why our human nature is to indulge in something or someone that's bad for us. Beauty is a powerful thing."

Drew didn't know if he was referring to her, him, or their criminal activities.

"Shall we?"

Legend offered a wave of his hand and Drew strutted to his door.

Inside the massive home revealed large columns, marble floors, and a huge floor plan. Legend guided her to his living area flanked with an enormous fireplace, bearskin rug, plasma TV, and a 16th Century art painting hanging on one huge wall. Drew strolled to the painting.

"A man after my own heart," she whispered. She felt him move behind her. The heat radiating from his person ran the length of her.

"Would you like something to drink," his baritone voice beat.

She twirled, finding him bearing down on her so close she could smell the minty scent coming from his breath. Without another thought, their lips met setting a dragon flame scorching her insides. Legend's lips trailed down her neck, his hands on course to her waist. With ferocity, he pulled her pants, aggressive and demanding. Her arms circled his neck and she allowed him to unclothe her.

His shirt flew across the room, then hers. Legend snatched Drew up and laid her down on the bearskin rug. He didn't miss a beat as his mouth found her breasts, licking and sucking her dark brown nipples. He moved down her russet skin and rid Drew of her jeans. His mouth took in her vagina in one succulent kiss. His tongue thrashed inside and out circling her labia in hungry strokes.

"Mmmmm," Drew moaned.

Her mouth hung open, her eyes sultry as one of the many orgasms she would have that night set on a cataclysmic path. Legend was the escape she so desperately needed and for now, she would relish in him.

The next day...

Nia sat clutching the steering wheel to the Chevy Corsica she'd stolen the day before. Unfortunately, Nia was unable to make it to the homeless shelter in time to get a bed. That left her out on her ass with nowhere to go. Nia's survival instincts were quick to kick in, so while the elderly couple made their way into a grocery store, Nia snuck up on the older model car, hot-wired it and drove off. She reasoned that having somewhere to lay her head in the winter weather was imperative. Nia could die on the New York streets without shelter.

Her life was anything but smooth, but last night Nia was all set in a nice parking spot, to get a few z's before the morning sunrise, when her eyes fell on a man she'd spent the last three years evading. It was all Nia could think about since she'd watched him pull to the light and throw a snarky smile and wink in her direction. The thin hairs on her skin rose. He was a ruthless and insufferable human being. Manipulative at his core and cunning, to say the least. Nine years ago, Legend sweet talked Nia right out of her panties. Nia fell in love with him. As soon as she was comfortable, Legend turned on her in every way imaginable. He'd beaten her, threatened and controlled her, kept her away from family and friends. Nia tried to run away once, but he caught up to her and made her suffer tremendously by handcuffing her to the bed and allowing any manner of pervert to sexually assault her. Nia was bound to that bed for days; sustained on flat beer and every man's leavings.

Legend warned her that he would kidnap her twin sister and do the same. He would kill her son, her friends, her uncle, aunts, her entire family until there was no one left. Nia believed him.

Legend made his word bond for five, almost six long years. She was completely his, until one night, Legend beat her to such a bloody pulp that she had enough. While his guard was down, Nia snuck out fleeing him in the middle of the night. Nia knew Legend would tear up New York looking for her but she held high hopes that he wouldn't involve her family if she stayed away from them. And she did. Regardless of how much she missed them, how much she missed her son, Nia kept her distance. It had been three years and Nia thought she was in the clear, but she was mistaken. Drew managed to get in Legend's crosshairs and it was all her fault.

Now Nia was sitting across the street from the home previously shared with her son, sister, and cousin; her vision straight-laced, dazed and weighed down by the news she came to deliver. Nia's feet felt like bricks slipping into quicksand. Unmoving, she stared at the front door. Her knuckles ached from the tight grip she held on the steering wheel molding. She could call, Nia reasoned. It would keep the shock of her unkempt presence from watering down the real issue. Drew had fallen onto the radar of a psychopath who just happened to be a brilliant businessman.

Drew stretched, cozying her shapely figure into the warmth of Legend. Her eyes blinked then opened and a strong arm came into view. It was thrown across her waist, thick with muscles abound. The sun peeped through a set of all white drapes that hung from the window across the massive room. Drew listened to him breathe soundly. Last night, Drew put all of her woes to the side to spend the evening with a man she was hopeful would stick around for a while. And it felt great. A tiny smile came to her. Slowly, she turned full circle; her face mere inches from his.

"Good morning," he spoke with his eyes still closed.

"Good morning," she responded. "I didn't mean to spend the night."

"That's alright," he drawled. "I was hoping you would stay awhile." Finally, his eyes opened. "There's something I want to run passed you."

"I'm listening."

You don't really need your sister or your best friends."

Drew frowned, her eyes moving from side to side. Her voice became serious. "What are you talking about?"

He licked his bottom lip. "Remember last night when I said we could build a strong partnership?"

"Yeah..."

Legend paused letting his thoughts play out in his mind. "Let's just say, I had something else in mind when I sought you out. But you're a gem, a rarity, a one of a kind," he continued. "And I don't think you need Brooklyn, Symone, or Leah. With you, me, and Nia we're the whole package. Nia is just as good with lifting expensive merchandise. You see, I'm in business with more important people than the president. With us, you could be a billionaire." Legend stretched and reasserted his arm around her waist before continuing.

"I'm telling you this because I like your style. When it's time to handle business, you do, and when it's time to play," he grazed a tongue up her lips, "you play."

Drew was more than taken aback. Her curiosity led into panic way back when Legend mentioned their names. Remembering her voice, Drew rose to a sitting position and spoke. "How do you know about my family and you said Nia? What the fuck, Legend?"

Legend held his gaze on her. “Yeah, about that...”

When Brooklyn’s phone rang, she had just ended a heated argument with Symone. The night’s hours hadn’t settled the tension between the two.

“Hello!” Brooklyn fumed answering the call.

“Good afternoon, Brooklyn,” the male voice spoke thickly.

“Who is this?” Brooklyn retorted, uninterested in having a conversation.

“I need you to listen to me and I need you to listen good. I hate repeating myself. I have something you want and you have something I want. We’re going to make an exchange.”

“You don’t have anything I want,” Brooklyn snapped.

The phone shuffled around before Drew’s voice broke through. “Sis, we have a major motherfucking problem.”

“Drew?” Brooklyn screeched. “Hello!”

The phone was snatched from Drew’s ear. “Now that I have your attention, I want two things from you.”

“Who the fuck is this?”

"This is the man you're going to piss off if you don't shut the fuck up and listen," he barked. "Two things," he reiterated, "I want the 40 million dollars that was transferred into that offshore account yesterday for the Saliera. I also want my Nia back."

Brooklyn's throat went dry. "Nia?"

At the mention of her sister's name, Leah stood to her feet and flew to Brooklyn's side.

"Everything hidden always comes to light," Legend whispered.

"I don't understand, who is this, where is my sister and how do you know Nia?" Brooklyn shouted.

"You have 48 hours to complete my request. I'll call you back when your times up. Then and only then will you see your sister again."

"What?!" Brooklyn screamed. "Drew!"

The line died. Brooklyn whipped around with wide eyes.

"What is it?!" Leah yelled.

Brooklyn's gaze fled from Leah as the doorbell rang.

Chapter Fourteen

She was an absolute nervous wreck and considered retracing her steps, getting back in the Corsica and getting out of there as fast as she could. But the bell had been rung. Nia had run long enough. Now, it was time to face her worse fears, her demons, and her family. To make herself more presentable, Nia smoothed down her mangy mane, ran her hands across her layered clothing and used the tail end of a shirt or jacket, whichever one, to try and wipe layers of shame from her face. Her heart beat frantically in her now bony chest. Maybe if no one responded, she could turn around and leave knowing she gave it her best effort.

And then the door opened and Nia thought she would pee on herself. She wanted to see who it was but didn't want to look. That's why her head was hung low when Brooklyn opened the door.

"DRE-"

Drew's name was caught in Brooklyn's throat when it wasn't who she hoped was standing at the door. That would have made the previous phone call a bad fucking joke and they could laugh about Brooklyn getting pranked. But that's not what was going on; not at all. Nia lifted her head up only enough to where she could look up from under her messy hair to see her friends face.

Brooklyn and the woman standing at the door locked eyes. Nia, ashamedly; Brooklyn completely flabbergasted. Brooklyn couldn't find words and nearly lost her bearings as she held on tightly to the doorknob hoping it held her up. But as recognition of the woman standing in front of her took over, the door had to hold Brooklyn up, and brace her as she slid to the floor.

"Oh, my fuckin' Christ..."

Nia wasn't sure what to do; whether to run away or stay and help Brooklyn. Deciding on the later, Nia offered a stained smile as she knelt down to assist her friend, whose eyes remained wide. Hearing the commotion, Leah came to the door, not sure what to expect but prepared to fight tooth and nail if her family was threatened.

Once she got there, she saw Brooklyn pulling a Fred Sanford on the floor and some stranger bending over her.

"What the hell is going on," Leah declared, bracing just in case she had to whoop somebody's ass. She searched Brooklyn's upturned face in an effort to read her, but struggled as all she could see was wide eyes and an open mouth. And then she felt it. Even before their eyes connected, she felt it. Leah's heart began to swell, as the hole long since put there began to fill. When Nia looked up and found her twin's eyes, they both had a moment. The supernatural connection they shared from the womb was reinstated. Leah saw confirmation in her twins' eyes that the nightmares Leah had were Nia's reality. And Nia saw the life she'd been missing and so desperately wanted to be a part of.

But before either of them could verbally address each other, Nia's gaze was stolen by a figure standing innocently in the doorway. Brooklyn, who had regained a small bit of her composure, followed Nia's eyes. Leah didn't need to turn around. She knew James was standing there. Nia began to shake and her eyes welled with tears. She collapsed to the floor, joining Brooklyn. Words could not be found. She wanted to simultaneously greet her son and apologize for leaving him. Those words didn't escape her lips because in her heart, she knew, she was not his mother... Leah was...

It was only so much more trash talking Symone was willing to take. First, it was Brooklyn and then Drew and then Brooklyn again! Symone had had her fill. The only person who hadn't cursed her out in the last 24 hours was Leah, and of course Mason...

Mason...

Even though he was culprit for the problems with Brooklyn, Symone couldn't help it. When she said his name, when she thought about him and how he pursued her, she got giddy like a school girl. That was the damn problem. Too damn giddy. What hurt the most was that both Brook and Drew were right. She had compromised their identity and the ultimate mission all because of some damn man. If the shoe was on one of the other girls' foot and they did what she had done, Symone had to admit to herself that she would still be cussing they ass out. So why did she think she should be absolved of accountability in this situation?

If she was honest with herself, she deserved more than they dished out. So even though her feelings were hurt, Symone determined that she would fix the fuck up. She had to. Everything was on the line.

Symone needed some fresh air. Clearing her mind and focusing on a fix was necessary. She considered going to the coffee shop. Damn her hips. What she wouldn't give for a caramel macchiato, vente, with extra whip. When her phone buzzed, Symone rolled her eyes.

"They gone leave me the hell alone!"

Climbing in her car and closing the door behind her, Symone checked the phone that was still buzzing. The smile that teased her lips clearly indicated that the call wasn't from one of the girls.

"Hey you," she purred into the receiver.

"I need to see you," Mason replied, smiling equally as hard on the other end.

"No sir," Symone teased. "You've gotten me in enough trouble already."

"Give me a chance to fix it."

"And how do you propose to do that, Agent Fuller," Symone asked with syrupy sweetness. She dismissed the voice in her head that shouted 'trouble'.

"Meet me, thirty minutes, at the spot."

The cautionary voiced yelled again, but Symone stifled the warning.

"See you there."

She stood there at perfect attention, like a guilty military soldier before court martial.

Her boss, Special Agent Jericho Jones, sat behind his desk and stared at Agent Stinson, refusing to absolve her of whatever she was feeling at the moment. He decided to let her sweat and try and speculate as to what he would say. He didn't offer her a seat although there were two vacant ones immediately in front of her. Agent Stinson was a good agent, but that was her biggest problem. She thought she was good; taking on too much of the arrogance her partner so effortlessly displayed. At least Agent Fuller had successful history to back up his arrogance. Stinson did not.

"Were you on official bureau business when you wrecked the car?"

His question was laced with self-incrimination and they both knew it. Being in a bureau vehicle and not conducting business was a 'no no'. Stinson could get written up for that. She offered the obvious answer.

"Yes, sir."

"Hmmm..." he pondered. S.A. Jones rumbled through some papers on his semi-cluttered desk and retrieved what he'd been searching for.

"Are you sure, Agent Stinson?"

Brittany's nerves, already operating on overload, surged. What did he have on her? What was on the paper?

"Yes, sir," she replied, attempting to sound confident. "I am always taking care of business." She painted the scenario with a broad stroke, hoping it was sufficient to ward off any negative repercussions or at least to minimize them.

"Mmhmm," he murmured again. "Well, according to the log sheet, there was no sanctioned 'business' as you call it." S.A. Jones waved the paper in his hand. "Care to explain?"

Fuck!

Agent Stinson started to stammer. She knew better than to not log her actions. But she acted out of emotions when trailing Symone. How was she going to explain that to her boss?

"Sir, I know I didn't log it into the official form and I apologize for that. But, there has been something bothering me about this case since the beginning; so I took a chance."

"And where was your partner in all of this chance taking?"

This was the perfect opportunity to throw Mason under the fucking bus. As much as he'd hurt her in the past, Brittany could use this as leverage.

“Well, he had my back on this one, sir. He attended to the suspect to draw attention away from me.” Her mind said sell his ass out, but Brittany’s heart wouldn’t allow it.

“Oh really?”

“Absolutely, sir. Fuller is as dedicated to resolving this case as I am. After our mishap overseas, we have been working around the clock to rectify the situation.”

“I see,” S.A. Jones replied. He sized the agent up again; his eyes trailing her from the top of her head. Then, he leveled a fierce gaze that did not waiver.

“You are close to a fuckin’ demotion. You realize that don’t you, Agent Stinson?” Jones wasn’t looking for a response. “You got one more time to test the edge of my patience and your ass will be in the tombs clocking evidence bags. Do you understand what I am saying to you? You got one more time. Now, get the hell out of my office.”

“Yes sir,” Stinson uttered, relieved his chastisement wasn’t worse.

As she made her way to the door, Brittany’s superior got her attention again.

“Stinson,” Jones called out, leaning forward on his desk. The agent slowly turned around, praying her boss didn’t have second thoughts about her punishment.

"That car you wrecked, you are paying for the fix." Stinson nodded. Forming words with the course of adrenaline pumping in her veins was too difficult. She turned away and grabbed the door knob. But, clearly, Jones wasn't finished with her.

"And, tell your partner, if I don't have resolution on this case within the next 30 days, Im'ma have both your asses!"

Brittany made a quick exit. She felt relieved the situation hadn't been worse. Now she needed to talk to her fuck of a partner. He wasn't in the pit with the other agents, which was no real surprise given how he'd been behaving. Brittany whipped out her cell phone and speed dialed Mason's number.

When his phone rang, he contemplated whether or not to answer it. He was not in the mood for Brittany's shenanigans. Mason swiped the call and sent it to voicemail.

I know he ain't ignoring me? Brittany thought as she made her way through the station. She called the number again, just to make sure.

No sooner than Mason ignored the first call, his phone was ringing again. Without even considering it, he swiped again, sending the call straight to voicemail. He was on a mission and his partner was not going to mess this one up.

Brittany nearly stopped in her tracks when she was sent to voicemail again. Making her way to her car, Brittany jumped in and started it, revving the engine. An eerie smile crept across her face.

"I know exactly where you are, Mason..."

Mason arrived at the coffee shop a few minutes early. He wanted to have Symone's beverage already waiting for her, but not inside the coffee shop where other people and their conversations could distract them. Mason wanted to have a private conversation with Symone. Mason went into the shop, bought her favorite, and brought the drinks back to the car. They would talk there, where they couldn't be disturbed.

Symone didn't want to arrive too early to the shop. That would signal desperation and that's not the message she wanted to convey. She was eager to see Mason, but instead of pulling right up to the coffee shop, Symone hung back, a block over and waited for the time to tick down. It was better to be a few minutes late, make him wait for her with as much anticipation as she had for him. Symone decided to use the time wisely. She checked her hair and makeup in the rearview mirror to make sure they were perfect.

Brittany drove directly to the coffee shop. She knew he would be there. When she saw his car pulled near the back of the lot where there were far less cars, she pulled up behind it. She saw Mason coming out of the shop with more than one drink in his hand. Brittany waited until he was just about at his vehicle before exiting her own.

28 minutes ... Just a few more and Symone would make her way to the coffee shop. Reaching in her purse, Symone retrieved her favorite perfume and misted herself.

Mason nearly stopped in his tracks when he saw his partner getting out of her car.

"Don't look so disappointed, partner," Brittany said, sashaying over to him. "Looking for someone else I take it?"

Mason didn't immediately respond. This was not what he had in mind.

"What's so urgent, Stinson," he replied impersonally.

"I just saved your ass," Brittany chirped. "That's what's so damn urgent."

"What the hell do you mean?"

Brittany positioned herself where she could see the entrances to the parking lot. She turned Mason by her approach, knowing he would recoil the closer she got.

"I just got through meeting with the boss, and he ain't happy with either one of our asses right now."

"Oh, what you really mean is that he ain't happy with your ass," Mason rebuffed.

"I knew you would think that," Brittany began. She spotted a familiar vehicle slowly making its way down the parking lot. "Yeah, he chewed my ass about the car, but he also wanted an explanation as to your whereabouts and why you were on scene."

Mason hadn't considered that part of the equation.

"So what did you tell him?"

Brittany moved again, causing Mason to back up to his car.

"I told him you had my back." Out of the sight of the approaching car, Brittany used one hand to lift Mason's free hand to her waist and hold it there.

Symone thought she saw Mason and made her way to him. She was surprised when she saw his partner there, too. Symone slowed the car even more.

"Oh you did," Mason replied, trying to remove his hand from Brittany's grip.

“I sure did,” Brittany purred. “Don’t you think you owe me a thank you?” She was smiling and her eyes were beaming.

“Thank y—“

Before Mason could fully get the words out of his mouth, Brittany pushed passed the drink tray, planting her full lips on his. Mason had no place to go. His car held him steady. Brittany pushed her tongue into his mouth and held him firm against his resistance.

Symone stopped short. Her mouth fell open.

“*Son of a bitch...*” Symone uttered, as her heart sank.

But she wanted him to know she was there.

As Mason pulled away, Brittany smiled even harder as Symone’s car came into view. Mason followed Brittany’s eyes and his gaze landed on Symone who paused her vehicle in front of him long enough for him to see her.

“... Damn...”

Chapter Fifteen

"Would you like something to drink?" Legend circled the bar and popped the top on a bottle of scotch.

"You can cut the shit. You've revealed who you really are. You got everything you wanted out of me. There's no need to act like you really give a damn what I want." Her words were heated, and her blood simmered to a boil.

Everything Drew found out about the man she'd lain with made her gut churn. Revolted and in danger of emptying the contents of her stomach, Drew glared at Legend.

A crooked smile adorned his lips. "You know, things don't have to be this way." He held a short glass out to her half filled with scotch on the rocks.

"I don't get it. If you were going to steal our money, why didn't you just take the Saliera? Why go through the exchange and transfer of funds from your clients, when you could've just taken it and sold it yourself?"

Legend's eyes twinkled with mischief. "Paper trail..." he drawled. "When Brooklyn... that's her name, right?" He smirked. "When Brooklyn brings me cash, there will be no trace of my hand ever touching this transaction."

Drew shook her head in disbelief. "How the hell do you suppose she'll bring you cash? With the amount you asked for, I can guarantee it won't be cash, but a direct transfer. So, your paper trail plan won't work." Drew held a smug smile.

Legend's smiled widened. "You're right, but you're wrong about one thing. Drew puckered her lips in defiance waiting for him to continue. "There won't be a connection between me and the Saliera." Legend shrugged. "That's all that really matters."

"You've got it all figured out, huh? So this is what you do, steal from your clients?"

"I'm not stealing from them, I'm stealing from you."

"You never stop to think what would happen if word got back to your clients of your shady dealings?"

The twinkle in Legend's eyes went out. "No one would dare do that, sweetheart."

"And why is that, sweetheart? Because you're the big bad wolf?"

His smile returned. "Yes I am, baby," he growled. "And you're little red riding hood." Legend licked his lips. "And if you don't mind me saying so, you ride one helluva hood, too."

Drew's forehead creased; her mouth turned down into a frown. She hated the way her body reacted to his words. What the hell was wrong with her? So what he rocked her world. Drew had lost count of the many orgasms she released last night, but Drew wouldn't tell his janky ass that.

"You're disgusting," Drew spat.

"And you like it," he responded getting in her face.

She pushed off him and walked around Legend to claim a seat at the bar.

"So you're just going to keep me here until my sister brings you our money?"

"That's the idea."

"What If I try to leave, then what, you'll kill me?"

Legend's jaw tightened. "I'll fuck you until your pussy bleeds, but then you might enjoy that as well."

Drew fought hard to control the horror that oozed through her.

"You're a lunatic! How'd I ever see anything else?"

Legend poured another round of scotch in his glass.

"Because we belong together, baby. It's the way of the universe. Even if you hate to admit it, our stars align. Tell me, haven't you always felt excitement in your life, lacking? Don't you want to take life by the balls and create your own path?"

He glided towards her, his steps slow and even. "Haven't you wanted to fuck, uninhibited, chained to the bed, like last night, or out in the wild like an animal?"

"I'd like to grab you by the balls and hang you upside down by them," Drew spat.

Legend laughed. "You see that shit right there? It makes me want you more. You should stay with us, Nia could use a sister wife."

"You're out of your mind. We haven't seen Nia in years! Who the hell knows where she is or what she's doing. Who even knows if she's still alive...?"

"No need to worry about that," Legend replied. The slick grin on his face was troubling. "She's still alive. I saw her last night."

Drew's eyes bucked. "What do you mean you saw her last night?"

"Trust me when I say, she's alive and well. Your sister will find out soon enough, and you better hope she finds out within the next 48 hours."

"Or you'll kill me?"

"You're too fun to kill, but I will have my way with you."

Legend walked back to her and Drew recoiled. He leaned in to whisper in her ear, “And you’ll love every minute of it.”

Symone put the car in reverse slowly turning back onto the road. She gave one last glance at Mason before pulling off. “Stupid,” Symone chastised herself. The phone in her lap rang immediately. It was him. Without hesitation, Symone swiped the screen sending the call to voicemail. Within seconds it rang again, and again, she sent the call to voicemail. A notification came through from Brooklyn. Symone rolled her eyes. The last thing Symone wanted was to deal with her. Brooklyn made it abundantly clear that Symone was fucking up and Symone was on the verge of saying to hell with it all.

Slowly, the car rolled to a stop at a red light. Symone opened the message:

Emergency at my place! Get here now!

The fine hairs on Symone’s neck rose. “Emergency?” she muttered putting a firm foot on the gas pedal. A horn blew as she hit the corner. “*What the hell could it be now?*”

Confusion set in on James's face as he stood in the doorway. His eyes roamed from his mom to the woman who now sat on their living room couch. They had the same mouth, nose and although the other woman had dark circles, her eyes were the same as his mom's.

James glanced to Leah; tears streamed down her face. She was hurt, and he didn't understand why. Her sorrow made tears form in his eyes. Since the woman entered the house, everyone seemed distant.

"Mom," James cried out taking steps into the room. She stood in front of the woman, with her hand covering her mouth. James slid his arms around Leah. His voice and warmth bringing her out of shock.

Leah dropped down to her knees. "Baby, your friend Daniel just got a new game system for making honor roll for the third time this year. Why don't you go next door and play it with him?"

James wiped the tears that threatened to fall from Leah's eyes. He turned his sights on Nia getting a good look at her. "Why do you look like my mom?"

Leah trembled. She could only hold on to her distress for so long, and James was making it hard for her. Nia opened her mouth to speak.

"Baby," Leah chimed in bringing James's focus back to her. "She's a distant relative, that's why. Go on now, or I'll change my mind, and you can wash the dishes."

It was meant to make him run for the hills, but James was worried about his mother. He wiped her eyes again and fell into her embrace placing soft kisses on her cheeks.

"I love you mom," James said.

Leah beamed. "I love you too, baby."

"If you have any trouble, I'm just next door," he reminded her.

"Okay big man, I'll make sure to remember that."

They all watched him leave the room. When the door opened James murmured, "Hey Auntie Symone."

"Well hey to you too, James. Why the long face?"

James shrugged and moved passed her. Symone, with a frown on her face, watched him go. He knocked on the neighbor's door, but it opened before his knuckles could complete the rhythm.

The door closed and Symone entered the living room. Her gaze fell on Brooklyn first. "What's wrong with James?" It was then that she looked to Leah and the frail looking woman on the couch.

As recognition set in, a ripple slid down Symone's spine, and her eyes bucked. "Oh...my...God."

Symone didn't move another inch, her mouth dropped, then closed trying to formulate words that just weren't coming to her.

"I know my presence is startling," Nia initiated. "But there's a bigger problem that needs to be dealt with now rather than later."

Symone's mouth was still opening and closing.

"Drew," Brooklyn whispered. She held her head and bent forward. "The man on the phone said he wanted the forty million dollars we received for the Saliera and he wanted Nia back within 48 hours."

Symone took a step towards Brooklyn. "What the fuck are you talking about?"

Brooklyn heaved a heavy sigh. "The guy Drew used as the middleman for the transaction is now holding her hostage. We have to hand him over the forty mill we got for it and," her eyes went to Nia. "He wants Nia back."

A sob broke, and Leah slunk to her knees. She fell back to her butt and pulled her legs into her chest, wrapping her arms around them. Everyone moved to console her.

"It's over, we're done," Leah whispered.

"Why are we done?" Brooklyn stammered.

"What do you mean?" Leah cried out. "We've got to go to the police! He has Drew!"

"And what will we tell the police? That we're the criminals they're looking for, and a man is holding one of our own hostage?" Brooklyn chided. "Think about what you're saying Leah; I know you're in shock but don't be ridiculous."

"This is way past shock, Brooklyn! He has your sister! What are we supposed to do, give him back my sister in exchange for yours?"

"Whoa," Symone put her hands up. "Everybody calm down."

They all focused on her hoping she had a better plan.

"Time out," Nia spoke up. Her eyes wandered from Brooklyn to Symone, then her sister. "You're the criminals the FBI is looking for?"

"Oh yeah," Symone drawled. "That would be us." Nia cupped her mouth.

Symone exhaled continuing the conversation. "Okay, we have forty million for the Saliera, right?"

"Yes," Brooklyn responded. "It was worth fifty, but we could only get forty on the black market for it."

"Okay, how much did we get for the bank heist?"

"Ten million," Brooklyn confirmed.

"Maybe we can make an exchange, Drew for the fifty million we have."

"That would be everything! We'd have to start over from scratch!" Brooklyn fumed.

"He has your sister; it's our only option."

Brooklyn folded her arms. "What if he doesn't go for the extra ten million?"

"I'll go back."

Nia's voice broke through their conversation. "It's me he wants. Drew shouldn't suffer because of the choices I've made." Nia rose to her feet. "I'll go back," she confirmed.

Leah jumped to her feet. "The hell you will! I've had you back in my life all of two seconds. You're not going any damn where!"

"Nia where have you been?" Symone asked concerned.

"With Legend, it's a long story, one we don't have time for. Just know he's an evil man, and I don't want Drew with him any longer than she's already been."

Tears sprang from Leah's eyes, and her head shook. "You're not going back, I don't give a damn what he says," she stuttered. "If we have too, Symone will get Mason involved. He's infatuated with her. He'll help without us going to jail or some shit right, Symone?"

Symone took a step back her mouth agape. "I...um..." she tugged at her shirt, "I don't know if that's the best move."

"But it is a move!" Leah said.

"Hell, if you're going to fuck him, better make sure it's worth it, right?" Brooklyn injected.

Symone rolled her neck and sat a glare on Brooklyn. "You should worry about who you're fucking, how about that, Brook!"

"No, we're not doing this right now!" Leah spoke again. "This is a play we may have to use."

Symone rubbed the back of her neck. How in the hell would she get Mason involved without revealing their hand? Her head thumped. Symone held her hands up in surrender. "Let's just try the money exchange first and see what he says."

Leah spoke to Brooklyn, "Do you have the number he called from?"

"He called from Drew's phone."

"Okay call it back," Leah ordered. A vibration slid through her. Devastation set in her bones. Leah put her sights on Nia. Timidly, Nia stood close to her with sad eyes weighed down by a stressful life.

"You have something for me?" Legend answered.

"Where's Drew?" Brooklyn asked.

Drew's voice came through the speaker. "I'm fine, Brooklyn."

"See," Legend offered, "She's fine. Now that you've called this phone I assume you have something for me."

"We don't know where Nia is," Brooklyn spoke. "The best we can do is give you ten million more dollars in exchange for Drew. It's all the money we have."

"No Brooklyn, don't give him shit!" Drew shouted in the background.

Legend chuckled, "Your sister over here, she's a feisty one, ain't she?"

"Will you take our offer?" Brooklyn asked getting down to business.

"I'll tell you what, since I know Nia is a coward and wouldn't doubt that she'd continue to run, I'll make you another deal."

The girls waited impatiently for him to continue.

"Seventy million total and she's yours."

Leah's mouth dropped.

"Seventy million!" Brooklyn screamed. "What part of fifty million is all we have, don't you understand? Where the hell are we supposed to get twenty million more?"

"I guess you better figure it out. It's either that or my original deal, forty million and Nia." The line died.

"Hello!" Brooklyn screeched.

Leah began to pace. "We're going to have to rob some banks. We have to do it."

"We can't rob banks back to back. It would take hours of surveillance to get that kind of cash let alone we're down one woman!"

"What about the heist in Africa you were working on?" Symone added.

Brooklyn looked to her. "We're still a woman down, and that heist would take about a week at the earliest to take on. Have you guys even studied the blueprint for the mission?"

"I have," Leah said.

They looked to Symone. "Yes, I have."

"The time issue is still a problem. We can't leave Drew in the hands of that maniac for a week!" Brooklyn was about to pass out. She held a hand out to steady her weight against the wall.

"We may not have a choice," Symone injected.

"How quickly can it be done if you have the manpower you need," Nia's soft voice asserted. All eyes went to her.

"No," Leah said. "Hell no. You're not in shape; you can't."

Nia held a soft eye on Leah. "I can do more than you think, sis."

"Honestly, we don't have time to debate this. Hell, we don't have time for anything. What's it going to be, the bank heist or the jewelry heist?" Symone asked.

Their eyes roamed from one to the other; neither of them quick to respond.

"If we do the jewelry heist," Brooklyn offered, "Then at least we can recoup some of the money we're losing. It's the Steinmetz Pink Diamond, valued at twenty-five million. And to answer your question Nia, yes we could use your help, but we don't want you to think you have to help because of this psycho. You'll need to be on your A game."

"Don't worry about that, just tell me the plan."

Chapter Sixteen

"You're a fuckin' idiot," Drew said, leaving Legend where he stood.

"And how's that," Legend inquired. Feisty was cool but disrespect? That's some shit he wouldn't tolerate. He needed to determine if Drew was staying on the right side of things before he acted.

"Just so typical," Drew continued, making her way over to the couch and sitting down. She had to make this situation work to her advantage; take Legend out of the driver's seat without cluing him in on the fact that he'd been dethroned.

Legend took a long sip of the scotch left in his snifter and leaned against the bar.

"Typical?"

"Like a regular nigga on the street," Drew contended.

Legend chuckled then sat his glass on the bar.

"Have you looked around?" He lifted and opened his hands, looking around the space they were in, encouraging Drew to do the same.

"Ain't shit typical," Legend replied confidently.

"Yeah, it kind of is," Drew suggested, pulling her legs underneath her and sitting further back on the couch. Her dismissal intrigued Legend.

"Do you really think I'm impressed with things, Legend?"

She wasn't. That's part of why he liked her. Legend knew the same tired games he played a million times before wouldn't work on Drew. They may have worked on Nia; she was naïve and infatuated. Drew, not so much.

"I stole a fifty million dollar salt shaker; some shit most folks can't even pronounce. I did that, me! So do you really think this three, four million dollar spread you got here impresses me?"

"So, typical... what's with that?" Legend asked.

"You just like the corner man on the street. You think you the boss, sitting in the cut making moves. But your mentality, how you do business? This ain't nothing but some polished off street shit. You still acting like the nigga on the corner."

"The fuck?"

"Oh, you offended? Why is that, Legend? Cause the shit I said hit home?"

Drew waited and watched Legend as he thought about what she said. One thing about men that Drew learned the hard way. As much shit as they talk about a girl being crazed over them, they talk like that when they sprung. Legend was sprung, he liked her as much as he thought she liked him. Now, it was time to play the playa at his own game.

"Naw, it didn't but, Im'ma let you make your point." Legend crossed his arms over his masculine chest.

"Fine. Here's the point." Drew unfolded her legs and leaned forward on the couch.

"You still tryna come up. It's short-sighted, like the lil' boy on the corner slinging rocks. Your plan is short-sighted and shows where you are vulnerable. See, if you were dealing with a man, the vulnerabilities I see, he wouldn't even pay attention to. But I'm a woman. A smart one at that. I see through the bullshit, and I'm calling you on it. Your plan lacks vision and foresightedness. You have no real long-term plan of execution. Your car may be Manhattan, but your skill set, boo, that shit still East Harlem."

Legend found himself listening to something he wanted to dismiss. He gave no thought to his hand being on his chin but Drew recognized that she had his wheels spinning. Something she said hit home, and now he was the one wondering.

"Had you handled this right, instead of showing your weak ass emotional attachments, you wouldn't be trying to extort money from us in exchange for someone you know you can control. What's up with that?"

She watched him as he stroked his chin and started to shift his weight from one foot to the other.

"Right," Drew continued. "You acted out of emotion. You showed your hand. It's not about the money, Legend, you and I both know that. It's all about the power and control you lost when you lost Nia."

Drew eased off the couch, and when she did, Legend stopped pacing. She made sure to connect with him, holding him with her eyes, refusing to let go. Drew saw his eyes soften and she moved closer. By the time she finished walking, they were within kissing distance.

"You tried to make me your bitch, when you should have made us your partners. What? You thought me and Nia was the same? That I would be scared of you? That you could just exchange one of us for the other? That you could control me like you did her?"

When Drew reached back and slapped his handsome face, hard enough to draw blood from his lip, Legend was stunned. His first inclination was to strike back, but he met her eyes and saw what attracted him to her in the first place. Drew was right. He did think that; that he could replace

Nia with one close to her. Being called on the carpet like that was sexy when it should have been an affront. Legend grabbed Drew by her balled fists, held tightly at her sides. She resisted, not knowing what to expect from him. This time, Legends' eyes didn't give him away. They were stern and firm. Drew thought she saw anger there. Her resistance increased. And then he leaned in and kissed her full on the mouth, and she opened hers to receive him. He fully expected her resolve and resistance to weaken, but it didn't.

"You know I like that shit, don't you?" Legend asked, speaking directly to her lips.

"I ain't Nia," Drew said, speaking directly back to his.

"You made that clear." Legend kissed her again, and this time Drew pulled back with her body despite the cries from her womanhood to allow his entrance.

"Come here, girl," Legend whispered, smiling. Drew was close enough to feel his manliness throbbing against her. Drew's resolve faltered. Her arms relaxed and when Legend was convinced her intention was not to strike him again, he let her wrists go in favor of cupping the back of her head with one hand wrapping the other around her waist, pulling her back into him. As Legend lost himself in her, Drew opened her eyes to ensure what she felt from him was not just game. His kiss was intentional. The hold he had on her was intentional.

...got him...

"I know we are all in crisis mode," Symone began still shaken from everything going on. "And I ain't trying to be funny, for real."

"Stop right there," Brooklyn broke in. "All them disclaimers you spouting, yeah, you are trying to be funny."

Even though seeing Nia was overwhelming and the fact that her sister had been kidnapped nearly knocked the wind out of Brooklyn's sails, she was like an elephant. Brooklyn didn't forget shit. Symone was still on her short list of asses to kick.

"If anybody needs answers, it's me," Leah chimed in, overriding the discourse Brooklyn and Symone were preparing for. Leah wiped the tears still falling from her reddened eyes. Disbelief was not even the word for how she was feeling; so many mixed emotions. She had to find the words. Nia felt it even before Leah started to speak. Their connection apart was strong. In the presence of each other? It was more like telepathy.

Even though Leah's voice was low, everyone in the room felt her intensity. Willingly or unwillingly, the floor was relinquished to her.

"Start at the beginning," Leah said. Her eyes didn't connect with anyone as she still sat like a scared child in the corner. But everyone knew she was talking to her twin.

"Now's not the time," Nia replied, looking in her sister's direction. "We have to see about Drew."

"You don't get to tell me that," Leah rebuffed. "So, start at the beginning, Nia... you owe me that much."

The tension was layered upon tensions already hanging like a thick cloud in the room.

"I promise, Leah, I will tell you everything but right now"

Nia's statement was stopped short.

"Promise? Did you say promise?"

Brooklyn looked at Symone. They both felt like they were intruders.

Leah could care less what Nia's response would be. Unraveling herself from the corner, Leah took her time standing up. When she turned and faced her sister, all evidence of sadness had been summarily replaced with anger. Leah played it cool.

"You remember the last promise you made to me?"

Nia looked up at her sister who was now lauding over her like a bully. Her natural predilection was to withdraw. She'd been hurt too many times by a bully. Nia still had pains from that last time. Leah saw her twin began to cower, but her anger didn't allow the response her broken heart intended.

Nia wanted to give her the answer she desired. Maybe it was too many punches to the head, too many black eyes, and backhands, but she couldn't remember.

"No, Leah, I'm sorry, I don't..."

Nia's eyes stung terribly as salty tears formed in them.

"I know you don't, Nia, 'cause you left without promising me anything! You left me! You abandoned me, and you didn't promise me anything!"

The bitterness Leah had been holding onto spilled out in heated words designed to make her sister feel the pain she'd felt. She wanted Nia to know just how hard it had been.

"You not promising made me make promises I wasn't sure I could ever keep."

Leah was crying. Nia's head was down, taking the tongue lashing. Symone sat slowly, afraid to move quickly. She didn't want to draw Leah's venom in her direction. Brooklyn watched the whole situation unfold. Seeing the twins go at it reminded her of the last fight she had with Drew. It hurt...

"I had to make promises to your son, our son, that I didn't know if I could keep. Nia, do you understand how hard that was? How hard that is? And now the courts are coming after..."

Leah stopped the conversation short. This was not the time to drag that whole situation up. But she couldn't unring that bell.

"What do you mean the courts?" Brooklyn was the first to ask, but Nia looked up when she heard what her sister said.

"It's nothing," Leah said attempting to be dismissive.

"This is not the time to hold out, Leah." Brooklyn left her place near the wall and walked over to where Leah stood. "What about the court?"

Leah shook her head. Thinking about it made her anxious. Her body started to shake involuntarily as an overwhelming sense of doom took over. Brooklyn grabbed Leah as she started to breakdown.

"They're trying to take my baby from me..."

Leah wailed and fell into Brooklyn's arms. Nia wanted to console her, but she wasn't sure if Leah was ready to receive a touch from her. Symone got ready to get up from the couch when her cell phone buzzed. He left another message. This was not the time, so she ignored it and went to Leah.

"They're trying to take James from me..." Leah said again. "What am I going to do?"

Chapter Seventeen

Three hours later

"See right there," Brooklyn pointed to the monitor. "There's a lapse in the time frame that the vault is opened, and no one comes back to it for thirty minutes."

Brooklyn rewound the tape and played it again. They were watching Brandon McGee, bank manager for Atlantic Bank of New York on the recorded tapes Brooklyn had been pouring over for days.

"Brandon goes into the vault every morning before the establishment is open to the public," Brooklyn continued to point at the screen so Leah, Nia, and Symone could grasp what she was saying. After Leah's confession about the court proceedings, they'd all had a chance to cry it out. Now Brooklyn was getting down to business. They had to get this money and make sure James stayed with them. No questions.

"When he goes in, there's a vacuum sealed bag tucked underneath his arms. Look!" Her fingernail tapped the screen as she paused the tape.

"Right there, you can barely see it and if you're just passing by, it's unnoticeable to the untrained eye. But because I've been studying this tape, I can see it sticking out, but here's the thing. The cameras inside the vault are on a loop during this time. Instead of shutting them all the way off, Mr. McGee has them set on a loop and that's his mistake. Because I'm the genius that I am, I trip the loop and the cameras continue to roll. Mr. McGee goes in, pulls out the vacuum sealed bag and stretches it."

Brooklyn played the tape so the girls could see step by step what she was talking about.

"He places it in a corner of the room next to a crate of bills. When he comes out of the vault it's opened for 30 minutes before he goes back in for an additional 30 minutes, where he stuffs the bags until there's no more room inside them, then vacuum seals them tight. Half of them lay on an empty crate, one on top of the other. The other half he puts in black duffle bags that sit in this corner. See those bags? They're stuffed with money. Then Mr. McGee locks the vault on his way out."

"So he's stealing from his own institution," Nia asked.

"It's not his institution. Yeah, he's the bank manager, but that's about it,

and he's most certainly robbing them blind."

Bent slightly looking at the tape, Symone stood upright with her hands on her hips.

"I don't know about this. I mean if he's already robbing the bank then wouldn't this be a risky job for us? And furthermore, he must have an accomplice. Bank manager or not, he won't be able to move those bags on his own. If he's this smart, a time and date have already been established to take the money out. It's real risky."

"No," Brooklyn said, "I see where you're coming from but, no one's aware he's doing it."

She looked from Symone to Leah then Nia.

"It's the perfect score because we can use him to our advantage and he's clever. I don't know why I didn't think of vacuum sealed bags myself."

"Probably because we've never thought about pulling off a heist this big," Symone countered.

"You know, if you don't want to do it, go find Mason, I'm sure he'd looove to be in your company," Brooklyn snapped.

"Hey!" Leah interjected, "That's enough, I'm sick of hearing you two fuss and fight!"

Leah turned to Symone. "You will have to lay low."

Symone frowned. "Lay low?"

"Yeah," Leah continued. "Mason knows your face. If we decide to take the bank instead of the Steinmetz Pink Diamond, then you can't traipse inside with us. It will seem too obvious that you're a part of this and you'll be in jail before midnight."

Symone's head dropped and she blew out a deep breath. "So what am I supposed to do? Twiddle my thumbs?"

"You'll be our getaway driver and you'll need to be good because with the load of cash we're going in for, if we're caught, none of us will ever see Drew or daylight again..."

Leah let her words drift and the ladies all caught her point.

"And you," Leah turned on Brooklyn.

"Yeah Symone fucked up, but stop acting like your Little Miss Perfect. I seem to remember you falling for a guy that was married last year," Leah snapped her fingers, "What was his name, Malcolm?"

Brooklyn's mouth fell. "We said we'd never bring that up again!"

"And we won't. I'm just reminding you that nobody's perfect, so get over this vendetta you have with Symone. What's happened has happened. Let's move forward. A lot of shit is going on and I don't know about you, but there's no need to add unnecessary layers of frustration to it." Leah sighed and everyone knew not only was she referring to Drew being taken, but the reappearance of her twin and the weight of the courts wanting to place James in the system.

Nia laid a gentle hand on Leah's back. "I'll do whatever you need me to. If that's coming to court with you, I'll do that. They can't take James from me. I'm his biological mother and he'll stay in your care. James will never know anything."

Leah offered Nia a compassionate smile. "We'll deal with it later. One crisis at a time. Right now, the main thing is getting Drew back."

Nia looked to Brooklyn.

"Are you sure doing the bank job is the one we want?"

"I don't see why not," Brooklyn replied. "Brandon McGee has done the hard work for us. At this point, it's only a matter of getting inside and getting out quickly."

"How long do we have," Nia asked.

This was the part Brooklyn knew would be tricky.

"Five minutes, give or take."

At the apprehensive look on Nia and Leah's faces, not to mention Symone shaking her head, Brooklyn added, "I know it's a tight timeframe, but most jobs like this are done within 90 seconds. The one we did at the beginning of the year took us all of 67 seconds to get in, get to the back and rob them blind. We can do this one in five minutes."

A cynical laughed came from Symone and Brooklyn held back fumes.

"What's so funny?" Brooklyn asked through clenched teeth.

"We need twenty million dollars! The heist we did was for $500 thousand and even then, it took a good amount of watching and waiting before we moved in."

Brooklyn rose to her feet from the chair she'd occupied in front of the monitor.

"Listen, we're doing this. The choice is not ours. We don't have the same amount of time we had in the beginning. I will not sit idly by while my sister is being held hostage by that lunatic!"

"We do have a choice!" Symone barked back. "We can take on the Steinmetz Pink Diamond heist. It will get us all the money we need and then some. You said it yourself!"

"I changed my mind!" Brooklyn roared. She shook with a force of anger, fear, and trepidation; scared to death what would happen to Drew if they did the diamond heist instead.

"It would take a week Symone! A week!" Brooklyn reiterated. "Then who would move it? We can't use Legend for obvious reasons! We'd have to find someone else and if it was your sister--"

Leah side-eyed Brooklyn. "If it was her sister, what? I don't remember you going to war to help me find Nia when she disappeared."

The comment slipped right out of Leah's mouth like she'd been waiting to say it.

Brooklyn turned to her, "How dare you..."

Nia stepped in quickly. "Guys, don't, please."

Her eyes settled on them all. "Tensions are high, I get that, but Leah, you just said, let's not tear each other down."

Everyone watched each other. The seconds of silence felt like minutes as they all went through their own storm of thoughts.

"Fuck this," Brooklyn spat.

She pushed past Symone and headed straight for the front door. Symone caught her by the arm and Brooklyn whipped around with the glower of a raging bull.

"Where are you going?" Symone asked.

"I'm going to get this money. None of you can stop me. I'm done talking! You're either with me or you're not."

Leah sighed and rolled her eyes. "You can't pull off a heist like this alone and you know it."

Brooklyn shook off Symone's grasp and held her arms out.

"Watch me."

Brooklyn didn't wait for any kind of response. She turned and walked right out the front door.

"Shit," Symone said chasing after her.

Nia looked to Leah. "We have to do this with her."

Leah didn't respond verbally, but with a curt nod, she agreed.

"That's it then; it's settled," Nia replied.

Chapter Eighteen

"Brooklyn wait! I'm coming with you!"

Symone rounded Brooklyn's Impala; sliding into the passenger seat. Brooklyn slammed the door and started the engine.

"Get out, Symone."

"I said, I'm coming with you. Now, don't fight me on this. Where are we going?"

"Get... out... Symone..."

Locking her door and folding her arms over her chest, Symone sat still refusing to exit the vehicle.

"I'm not playing games with you, Symone. You might not want to be in this car with what I'm about to do. Now get out. I'm not being mean, I'm saving your ass. Get out!"

Symone sat up off the seat locking eyes with Brooklyn.

"I said... I'm going with you. Now, if you want me out bad enough, I'm willing to watch you try it."

Symone wasn't getting out and Brooklyn would just have to deal with it. The back doors to the Impala swung open and Leah and Nia climbed in.

“We’re in,” they both said simultaneously. Nia and Leah glanced to each other. It had been a long time since they’d done anything together, much less speak at the same time. Brooklyn whipped around to them.

“There’s no going back,” she said.

“You’re the headliner behind this operation, Brooklyn, and although it’s imperative that we get Drew back, you have to have your head on straight. One slip up and it’s over,” Leah stated matter of fact.

Brooklyn rested in her seat, her shoulders slightly slumping. Her head fell back and she shut her eyes tight.

“You’re right, but just hear me out.”

They were all listening carefully, interested to know what Brooklyn’s plan was for grabbing such a huge haul of cash.

“In about twenty minutes we’re going to the bank to wait for Brandon McGee to leave at the end of his shift. We’ll follow him home and make note of his address. Tomorrow morning when he leaves for work, Symone, you follow his wife. Take note of what school the children attend, and where his wife is employed. As soon as you get the information, text it to me. Then, make your rounds to the bridge on 39th and wait for me to call you. The monitor’s range will pick up live activity in front and on the side of the bank, but because I'll have the cameras on a loop, you won't be able to see inside."

"Shit," Symone sighed.

Brooklyn exhaled. "Because Mason has also seen my face, I'll need to go incognito. I have a wig and sunglasses and we all know where the cameras are, so no looking up."

Brooklyn took her eyes to the rearview mirror. "Leah, I'll need you already inside. You need to walk in with Brandon and let me and Nia in the back door where there's a secondary employee entrance."

"How am I supposed to walk in with him?"

Brooklyn's voice rose. "Just let me finish."

Again, they were silent, listening to Brooklyn's plan.

"Every day the security guard is waiting at the door with Brandon McGee when he enters. But he will mysteriously get sick and they'll have to call in a temp."

When Leah opened her mouth to speak, Brooklyn shut her down.

"Don't ask me how he'll become ill. You don't want to know the answer to that."

That shut Leah's mouth, but her brows were still furrowed as she stared back at Brooklyn through the mirror.

"You will be the security guard that morning. I have a uniform for you."

"Isn't there an officer on duty?" Leah asked.

"There is and you'll have to stay."

"What?!"

"You'll be completely exposed because you're playing the role of a temp. They won't have your name but they'll have your face. So, you'll continue to play your role until the end of your shift or when the police finish questioning you."

Leah didn't look optimistic and Brooklyn turned in her seat to face her.

"I know this is not ideal, but we have to do this. Remember when we did our first heist? Symone pretended to be a bank customer placing a deposit?"

Leah knew where this was going, but that didn't mean she had to like it.

"This time it's your turn." Brooklyn readjusted in her seat.

"We'll need another car. Symone is our second stop, where we'll switch the money and transport. I'll take care of that. I've also been working on a mechanism. I've tried it three times and it's worked. Basically, once you get in Leah, Brandon will explain to you what your job and duties are that morning. You'll make rounds, going from one end of the bank to the other, making sure nothing's awry. The police officer sits up front where he can watch incoming and outgoing traffic. But before the doors are opened, Brandon will make his way to the vault. When he does that, let him linger. We need him to put more money in bags, so we'll have less to do. When he leaves the vault, the doors to the branch will open and the day will begin, business as usual. I'm going to trip a switch which will allow me to set off the ATMs in front of the bank. The commotion will draw the police officer's attention along with any other members of the bank including Mr. McGee. This is when you let me in. While they're busy trying to disperse the crowd that will surely run to the ATMs for the free money, Nia and I will come in and help you grab the bags of cash."

"Do you have any idea how much it is?" Symone asked.

"Not exactly, but by the looks of what he's stuffing, it's at least two to three million."

"That's not enough," Symone groaned.

"I know, but like I said before, I don't know how much it is exactly. Could be five or 10 million for all I know. Whatever it is, we're taking it. The biggest part of this job will happen from the main server. Like you pointed out Symone, two or three million isn't enough," Brooklyn sighed. "I'm going to hack their system and send a wire transfer for the full twenty million."

Everyone was quiet as they waited for Brooklyn to proceed.

"This will not be as simple as it sounds," Brooklyn admitted.

"I'd like to point out," Leah said raising a finger, "That none of this sounds simple, especially the part where you wire transfer twenty million dollars."

Brooklyn pressed her lips thinly together and nodded her head up and down slowly.

"The first half of this mission is easy breezy if we all stick to the plan. However, it's going to take me at least ten minutes to hack the bank's system. I've already tried and their internal system has a plethora of backdoors. Going into the wrong one would trigger an alarm, and it can only be done on the bank's server."

"Ten minutes?" Symone said, "We only have five, Brooklyn."

"Don't you think I know that?"

"Then how are you going to get it done?"

Brooklyn hesitated before answering. "I've been practicing the bank's code. I can only get so far before I'm rerouted offline. That's why it has to be done on the bank's internal server. My thought is, being on the bank's internal server, it won't take as long."

Brooklyn turned to them.

"I know you don't want to hear this but here it goes. If I get caught... run."

"Bullshit!" Symone said.

"What type of foolery is this, Brooklyn?" Leah yelled.

Brooklyn turned back around and started the engine. She checked the dashboard time and backed into the street, heading towards Atlantic Bank of New York.

"We have to prepare ourselves for the worst. We do it with every heist."

"Not like that!" Leah said.

Brooklyn glanced through the rearview mirror at Leah.

"What do you propose? That we all get caught? Then what happens to Drew, the pharmaceutical company, our land? You can't give up if I'm caught. There's too much on the line."

"How about none of us get caught," Symone said.

"I said, in the worst-case scenario."

Brooklyn crossed the highway and rode at speeds of eighty miles an hour. It took them forty-five minutes to make it to the bank where Brooklyn pulled to the curb across the street and parked. She opened her door.

"Where are you going?" Leah said alarmed.

"Calm down, it's still business hours, I need to feed the meter or we'll get a ticket."

Leah breathed a sigh of relief. She knew all too well about desperation when a family member was in trouble.

"I'll feed the machine, I'm the closest to it," Symone said getting out of the Impala. Reaching into her pocket, she pulled out a few quarters and fed the machine. The passenger door rocked as she crawled back inside and shut it.

"I have a question," came Nia's timid voice. All eyes turned to her. "If you're going to wire transfer the full twenty million, why are we taking the money from the vault?"

Brooklyn, Symone, and Leah eyed one another.

"Do you want to tell her?" Brooklyn asked Leah.

Leah turned to Nia and caught her up on how the pharmaceutical business their parents co-owned was in trouble.

"Then we found out our farmland is up for auction. To make a long story short we need, 75.4 million dollars to keep the land and save the company."

Nia's eyes bugged out as she did the math. They would have to start completely over if they handed the money over to Legend. Being with Legend, Nia knew quite a lot about assets with different companies. The pharmaceutical business was worth billions. Nia didn't know one company in the drug industry worth any less. What surprised Nia was the debt their family owed. It meant they were practically bankrupt. A sadness fell over her.

Her family had endured stringent hardships and she wasn't around to help them or her son. But things would be different now. She would do whatever it took to help; even if this heist didn't work and she had to give herself over to Legend. James was better off with Leah, anyway. Leah had made it this long without her; Leah could make it even longer. Nia's sight went to Brooklyn. The strain on her face told Nia that Brooklyn would surely break if Drew didn't come back. Nia hated to think what Legend would do to Drew every sickening moment she was in his presence.

"Here he comes," Brooklyn spoke up, straightening her posture in her seat.

Symone, Nia, and Leah took their gazes to the front doors of the bank. Brandon McGee stumbled out and walked to the employee parking lot that sat attached to the side of the building. Brooklyn put the Impala in drive and waited for him to exit. When he did, she allowed a few cars to pass before she trailed him. Brandon lived in the upper part of

Manhattan. The neighborhood was clearly out of his price range; with manicured lawns, carved bushes that sat around each house, and fancy sculptures announcing the wealth of the district. Brooklyn knew this area well. She'd dated Malcolm for a year and spent a lot of time here, but that was before she found out he was married. Brandon's home didn't have a gate surrounding it like most of the homes did. But it was palpable he was keeping up with the Joneses.

"Grab this address," Brooklyn said as Symone whipped out her smartphone and typed the address in her notepad.

Brooklyn glanced to her. "You're supposed to use the burner phones."

"I don't have one on me. This is just temporary."

Brooklyn reached over to the glove compartment and pulled the latch. It sprang open revealing several burner phones. Symone lifted a brow.

"I never leave home without one."

Brooklyn made a U-turn and left the neighborhood. While she was giving a lesson on being safe, she needed to get her personal vehicle out of this area.

"Get some rest tonight. Tomorrow, we take Atlantic Bank of New York."

Chapter Nineteen

The shrill of Symone's alarm clock snatched her out of dreamland and it was a good thing, too. She'd found herself stretched underneath Mason as his toned physique glided across her warm flesh. Shaking off the wet dream, Symone reached over, laying a heavy palm on top of the blaring device. The clock read four a.m. She could settle to get a few more z's, but she wouldn't. Pulling herself to a sitting position, Symone tossed her legs over the bed taking in a few deep breaths. Her eyes scattered around the room taking in the amber and white colors that accentuated the dated furnishings. This could be the last time she set eyes on this room if things didn't go well today.

"Now that's no way to start the morning," Leah said.

Symone didn't turn to her right away.

"You seem indifferent about this heist, why?"

It was then that Symone turned to Leah standing in the doorway casting a shadow over the entrance of the room.

"You don't really need to ask me that, do you?"

Leah sighed. "You have to think of this job like all the others, if not, you'll slip up and we both know that can't happen."

Symone stood, stretching her limbs and rotating her shoulders. Last night, the four women went back and forth over every detail about their impending heist until they were blue in the face. Symone dragged herself off to bed shortly after eight p.m., needing to get as much rest as possible.

"Brooklyn never came back."

"What do you mean she never came back?"

Leah followed Symone into the bathroom. "She said she was going home to get some things and she never came back."

"And you believed she would?" Symone shook her head in disbelief.

"Yes, I asked her if she was coming back and she said she would. Maybe she wanted to be alone," Leah suggested.

"But she doesn't need to be, I'm worried about her." No matter how they fought, Symone loved Brooklyn.

Symone ran warm water in the sink and pulled out a toothbrush from behind the medicine cabinet.

"We've got other things to worry about. Let's keep that list short and just get through the day."

Leah frowned. "What's wrong with you?"

Symone mumbled as she brushed her teeth. "I don't know what you're talking about."

Leah squinted at her. "What's that tone I hear in your voice?"

The doorbell chimed and both Symone and Leah whipped around.

"That's probably Brooklyn," Symone mumbled continuing to brush her teeth.

Leah walked away to open the door. A cool breeze flew in and Brooklyn stood on the other side of the threshold dressed down in a pair of blue jeans, black Reeboks, a black t-shirt to match and a shoulder-length black wig.

"Well you're looking the part," Leah said.

Brooklyn rolled her eyes. "Tell me about it." She pushed past Leah going straight for the dining room with a book bag on her shoulder.

"Where's Nia?"

"Here," Nia's soft voice sounded. Both Leah and Brooklyn turned to her and Brooklyn smirked.

"I guess today you're my twin," Brooklyn said, looking Nia up and down, in her blue jeans, black shoes, and black shirt.

"It seemed to be the most obvious choice," Nia said.

"What happened to you last night?" Leah asked Brooklyn.

Brooklyn brought her attention back to Leah. "Nothing, I got home and decided I wanted to stay. Is there a problem?"

Leah watched her closely for a minute. "I suppose not."

"Where's Symone?"

"Getting ready. What do you have there?" Leah asked, questioning the book bag.

Brooklyn hauled the bag onto the table and unzipped it.

"One for you," she said to Nia, "and one for you," Brooklyn said to Leah.

"Why are we carrying weapons?" Symone asked walking into the room.

"Yes, why, Brook?" Leah seconded; staring at the 360 handgun that now sat in the palm of her hand.

"Just in case," Brooklyn said.

"We've never used guns before. Our operation is not like any others. There's no point in carrying one because neither of us is going to use it." Leah looked around the room. "Right?"

No one said a word and Leah's gut tightened. "Guys!"

"We won't hurt anyone," Nia said. "But it's good to have them if only for a scare tactic. It will keep people in their place, trust me."

They all stared at Nia, each having their own thoughts about what she could've possibly been a part of for the last eight years.

"Fine," Leah said. "But I won't need one since I'm an employee and all."

Symone turned the gun back and forth in her hand and pulled back the handle then flipped the safety securely locking it.

"Just in case," Brooklyn reiterated. "Are we ready?"

"Let's get this over with."

Symone sat the gun at her back and they filed out one behind the other.

Atlantic Bank of New York

6 AM

"Good morning, you must be Sarah," Brandon McGee said as he held out a hand to Leah.

"Yes sir," Leah took his hand in hers for a shake.

Brandon fumbled with a set of keys. "I'm sorry to call you in on such short notice. Harry, the guard that usually comes in with me, is sick. Happened at the last minute."

Finally, Brandon slid the key into the bank doors and held the door open for her.

"After you," he said.

"I'm your security," Leah replied. "Maybe you should go in first."

Brandon perked up. "You're right! After me," he said making an attempt at a joke.

Leah stepped in behind Brandon and closed the door, turning the lock while Brandon disarmed the alarm.

"Your job should go easy today. Follow me and I'll talk you through it."

Leah trailed behind Brandon as he pointed out the areas she would watch.

"We also have an officer on duty, so keeping an eye on things won't be totally up to you. Besides that, we have a pretty good security system."

"How so?" Leah asked.

"Well, if at any time the alarm is triggered, the cameras take immediate snapshots of everyone in the building. Also, the doors are automatically locked. Not I or anyone else can unlock them until police arrive."

"And how does this system know when the police arrive?"

Brandon chuckled. "New York's finest will have the code to shut the system down. One is sent to their headquarters as soon as the alarm is triggered."

Brandon stopped walking and turned to Leah. "But you won't have to worry about any of that. If Harry's better tomorrow, you'll only have to endure a day of the hustle and bustle of this place."

Leah smiled thinly.

"You can round the building here." Brandon continued his stride.

Leah kept her eyes on every detail of the bank.

"What's down this hall?"

"Oh, that's an employee entrance."

They walked down the hallway to a door that would unlock with the slide of a keycard.

"Some of the tellers don't care to come through the front door, so they enter here in back. The door can't be opened inside or out without this." He handed her a card. "Congratulations, it's your very own temporary keycard."

The back door opened and the officer strolled through. "Morning," he said to Brandon. The officer set his sights on Leah; a smile spreading across his lips. His tone became husky as he spoke. "Good morning."

"Good morning, Officer?"

"Oh, I apologize," Brandon interrupted. "This is Officer Myers. Officer this is Sarah Middleton. She'll be working in Harry's place today."

"Is that so?"

"Yeah, unfortunately, Harry called in sick."

"That is unfortunate, but you're prettier than Harry anyway," Officer Myers winked.

Leah pulled back that thin smile again.

"Well, I need to make my morning rounds. We'll open up in thirty minutes," Brandon injected.

The door opened again and more employees strolled through, all of them speaking one after another.

"Do you need help with anything?" Officer Myers asked.

"No, I think I can manage."

"I'm right up front if you need a helping hand. I can't be missed since I pretty much stand as still as a statue like this." Officer Myers stood with his shoulders back impersonating a statue.

It was all Leah could do not to roll her eyes.

"I get your point. If I need anything, I'll let you know."

Leah walked away from the officer trying to put as much distance between the two as possible.

Chapter Twenty

"Do you copy?" Symone said through the walkie talkie.

"Yes," Brooklyn spoke back.

Symone glanced at her watch. It was 6:30 a.m. Looking back to the monitor, she watched Brandon step to the glass doors and open the bank for business like clockwork. For the first fifteen minutes, activity was unusually low, but slowly customers began to enter the bank. The downtown street held its normal movement with an influx of traffic with every passing minute. In her sitting position under the bridge on 39th, Symone's feet balanced on her toes, and her leg shook with a steady nervous vibration; then it happened. Two White males passed the bank's ATM when money flew from the spout. A few women behind them gasped.

"Oh my God!" One of them said catching the young men's attention.

"It's spitting money!" Another woman yelled. The men's faces lit up in surprise and mischief.

The bills flew into the street getting caught up against the windshields of passing cars.

Motorists came to a halt as everyone began to realize money was falling around them. Pedestrians ran to the machine, arms out, stuffing every pocket and crevice they could. Jumping out of cars, people stopped traffic leaving it backed up past a green light as they too flocked to the falling bills.

Horns blared as the drivers stuck in the intersection swore while they leaned into their steering wheels. The police officer inside the bank ran out with Brandon hot on his heels. Their eyes widened at the disorder happening in front of their bank, and they ran to the crowd in an attempt to diffuse it.

Symone glanced back down at her watch. “Five minutes,” she murmured as she lie in wait for Brooklyn to make her move.

The back door opened and Leah stepped to the side. Brooklyn and Nia rushed through with empty duffle bags making their way straight to the vault. Once inside, they began to stuff them quickly.

“Toss me a bag!” Leah whispered.

"I need you to watch that door," Brooklyn said. She turned to Nia, "Snap out of it Leah! Fill your bags!"

"I've never seen this much money in my life," Nia said casting her eyes around the cash with wonder.

"And you never will again if you don't snap out of it!"

"This is incredible…" Nia said.

Brooklyn dropped her bag and walked to Nia laying a heavy hand across her face. The slap almost dazed Nia as she held her jaw with surprised eyes.

"Bitch you better get it together, my sister's life is at stake!"

"Brooklyn!" Leah screeched, offended at her audacity to strike Nia.

"What?!" Brooklyn turned to get in Leah's face. "What?" she growled gritting her teeth.

"This was a mistake," Leah said. "She's not ready. I knew she wouldn't be."

"No, I'm sorry, I'm ready." Nia grabbed her bags and quickly tossed the vacuum sealed money in them.

Brooklyn grabbed hers and went back to the task of packing the bags. Leah grabbed a bag and commenced packing it. After they'd gotten the bags filled to capacity, Brooklyn turned to Leah, handing her the bags she'd packed.

"Take these to the blue grand marquis sitting right outside the door."

"Where are you going?" Leah asked as Brooklyn walked away.

"To Brandon's office, we're running out of time." Brooklyn paused in her steps and turned to them one last time. "Remember what we talked about, if I get caught..."

"We know, just hurry up."

Brooklyn went out the door and made her way to Brandon's office. With the cameras on a steady loop and the tellers distracted, Brooklyn entered Brandon's office without interference. Quickly, she sat in the leather office chair, pulled the keyboard out and began typing.

Her stopwatch beep indicated three minutes had passed. Brooklyn hit a button to reset it for another three minutes. It would be past the five minutes they'd given themselves to get the job done, but Brooklyn wouldn't leave that office until she'd transferred the money.

She made it past the first two coded backdoors in the bank's system when Brandon rounded the corner into the office. An instant frown sat on his features as the two locked eyes. She looked somewhat familiar, but Brandon couldn't quite put a finger on where'd he'd seen Brooklyn before.

"Who are you and what are you doing in my office!"

Brooklyn's fingers never stopped moving. She was now past the third back door and in the process of transferring the dividends.

"You'll excuse me if I seem unbothered. I needed to use your computer."

"Young lady, I don't know who you are, but in ten seconds I'll hit a button that will lock this place down and bring NYPD in here, and you'll go someplace where you might never get out."

"Not without you."

"Excuse me?"

Brooklyn's fingers continued to move. All she had to do was finish this, enter the off-shore account number, and it was a done deal.

"Do that, and I'll be sure to let the police know that you've been stacking money back there in that vault for days now. Probably weeks looking at the amount you've managed to stash."

Brandon's eyes grew, and a small smile tapered Brooklyn's lips. Brandon recovered quickly.

"If you don't have proof then it's your word against mine. But believe me when I tell you, they're going to look into your black ass before they look into mine. He turned to walk out of the room when he heard a click behind him. Pausing his movements, Brandon turned slowly back to Brooklyn.

"I don't think you understand," she said holding the Smith and Wesson on him. "You don't have a choice. Now, unless you want me to blow your fat ass head off, I suggest you sit down, Mr. McGee, until I'm finished."

They eyed each other for a second longer than Brooklyn had.

"You wouldn't," Brandon said.

"Do you really want to try it with me?"

Another long second, then Brandon moved his heavy frame into the uncomfortable chair in front of his desk. Brooklyn kept the gun raised on him as she bent to tap the last of the numbers into the system and hit enter. The money began to transfer, and a loading bar sat on the middle of the screen. 30 percent, 40, 50, percent complete. Brooklyn was losing patience as she waited for the bar to reach 100 percent. When it did, her stopwatch beeped simultaneously. She tapped the device to shut it off and walked towards the door.

"It was nice doing business with you, and before you get any bright ideas, just know, I know where Mrs. McGee works and where CJ and Lindsey attend school."

Brandon's eyes grew wide.

"Oh and I'll take this," she said snatching his badge that held his keycard attached. Don't test me."

Brooklyn left the office quickly just as Leah rounded the corner.

Brandon came out of the room.

"Stop her!" He said to Leah as she passed. Leah and Brooklyn locked eyes and Brooklyn struck out running. Shit! Leah thought as she ran after her, playing her part of security guard. Brooklyn swiped the keycard pushing passed the back door and Leah followed her with Brandon right behind Leah.

"She's got a gun!" Brandon said.

"Wait here!" Leah shouted at Brandon. She exited the back door coming face to face with Brooklyn.

By this time, Nia made it to the car and sat in the passenger seat listening. She was ready to move out if need be.

"Shit, shit!" Leah repeated. "You've got to shoot me."

"What?!" Nia said leaning over the middle console listening to her sister. "No way Leah! What are you thinking?"

"We don't have time to debate this! You have to or he'll know I let you get away!" Leah glanced behind her frantic. "Do it! Do it now Brook!"

Leah threw her hands around Brooklyn pretending to tussle. Brandon exited the back door, his eyes wide as the girls fought. Brooklyn pushed her off and aimed her gun at Leah. Bang!

Nia screamed at the same time as Leah. Brooklyn jumped in the Grand Marquis and sped out of the parking lot; her hands shaking as she navigated through the dense traffic.

"I can't believe you shot her!" Nia cried. She tossed her tiny frame at Brooklyn scratching and swinging at her face. The Grand Marquis swerved as Brooklyn tried to fend Nia off and gain control of the car.

"You shot her! You shot my sister!" Nia continued frantically.

"I think I shot her in the leg! I had to!" A mist of tears clouded Brooklyn's vision. "Fuck!" she screamed beating the steering wheel. Brooklyn's cell phone rang, and she knew it was Symone.

When Brooklyn answered, Symone could hear Nia screaming in the background. Symone too had listened to Brooklyn shoot Leah from her safe spot in the van. Alarmed, Symone yelled, "What the hell happened?"

Brooklyn tried to get a hold of herself. "Are you under the bridge, we need to exchange vehicles now!"

"Yes, I'm here. What happened, Brooklyn?!"

"I'll tell you when we get there. We're on the way!"

Brooklyn shut off the phone and prayed Leah was okay.

Chapter Twenty One

"Talk and talk quick Brooklyn," Symone yelled as Nia and Brooklyn climbed into the van.

"Just get us the hell out of here, Symone," Brooklyn shouted, slamming the van door and tumbling inside with the weighted down bags of money.

"You shot my sister! How could you do that," Nia wailed, scrambling to the monitor's that were still watching the parking lot of the bank to see if she could see Leah.

"What the hell was that, Brook," Symone demanded as she moved the van as quickly through traffic as possible, without drawing unnecessary attention. Sirens wailed and police cruisers followed shortly thereafter making their way to the bank.

"That was not the plan! Not the plan at all, so start talking before I pull this damn van over. We can all go down."

Symone's threat was not idle. Seeing Leah hit the ground like that was too much.

"I didn't have a choice," Brooklyn spoke up.

"You did! You did!"

Nia was an emotional wreck. The anger and fear overwhelmed her, and she cried as she screamed. The van had gone too far away from the bank, taking the monitors out of range. Nia couldn't see her twin, but she felt her pain.

"No, I didn't!"

Brooklyn's heart beat loudly in her chest. All the repressed adrenaline from playing it cool in front of Brandon came on like a rushing wind, and now her senses were on edge.

"There had to be another way," Symone pressed, not willing to hear the bullshit from Brooklyn. But Symone kept the van moving.

"Don't you think if something else could have been done, I would have done it? I didn't want to shoot Leah, hell, it was her idea!"

Symone looked surprised. She hadn't been privy to the exchange between Leah and Brooklyn, so Brooklyn's account came as a shock.

"What," Symone asked unbelievingly.

"That's right," Brooklyn continued. "It was Leah's idea. She didn't want to blow the con."

The other two fell silent; Symone considering what Brooklyn said and Nia knowing it was the truth. The traffic light turned red and Symone stopped the van. She looked over at Brooklyn as she spoke.

"Think about it. If Leah would have let us get away with Brandon watching, he would have known something was up, especially after I threatened his ass. Nia, you heard her but you should have never been a part of this. You weren't ready and your little freak out in the vault made that clear. Symone, of course you didn't hear what was actually going on because you was too far away and the monitors have no sound. When we tussled, Leah made the suggestion, so we could get away and her cover would remain intact."

An irritated driver from behind the van's blaring horn demanded Symone's attention.

"Don't fuckin' blow at me," Symone screeched. "I will sit at this bitch until the light changes again... blowing at me..."

Brooklyn's eyes grew wide, hearing profanity spill from Symone's pristine lips. Nia snickered, hearing Symone and watching Brooklyn's facial expression change.

"What's so damn funny?"

"You never curse," Nia laughed. "At least not from what I remember. I guess some things do change."

"She still never does, Nia," Brooklyn chimed in.

“Well, I got plenty of reason to,” Symone replied, finally pressing the gas pedal and getting the van moving. “Leah shot. We don’t know how the hell she’s doing, Drew kidnapped… that’s… ugh…”

Whether from nervous energy or high anxiety, Symone’s expression tickled the girls and they laughed even more.

“This is so not funny, for real.”

“I know,” Brooklyn added, “but it’s better than crying.”

The laughter died, and the van fell silent. The levity of their situation rose up again, and the feelings were overwhelming.

“I trust Leah,” Nia said softly, leaning on their twin connection; something she was glad to be finally feeling again. “Although I don’t agree, if she said it had to be done, it had to be done.”

“She’s got her burner,” Brooklyn chimed in. “Let’s pray she calls.

“AAAHHH!”

“Oh my God,” Brandon yelled as he went to the aid of the guard, only after making sure the coast was clear. Leah rolled around in pain. She asked to be shot but didn’t anticipate just how much it would hurt. Crimson red blood soaked through Leah's pant leg and stained the socks she wore underneath. Leah writhed in pain as Brandon stood over her.

"Somebody call 911," Brandon yelled into the abyss. Even though the sound of the gunshot ricocheted from building to building, the melee in the front of the bank and the blaring alarm from inside the bank blotted out his cries for help. Brandon kept looking over his shoulder towards the door for someone to respond. There was none.

"AAHHHHH!"

Leah's eyes filled with tears in response to the sharp stabbing pain in her leg. As bad as it hurt, Leah was glad the girls got away. With no help in sight, Brandon sprang into action. He knelt in front of the security guard.

"Hold still," he suggested as he reached for Leah's soiled pants leg.

Leah quickly nodded, biting her lip to keep from screaming. Brandon could have been much gentler as he shoved Leah's pants up to see what the damage was, but he was so adrenaline-drunk, Brandon wasn't cognizant of his own strength.

"Shit," Leah screamed in response to the abrasive fabric rubbing against her fresh wound. Brandon's gut churned as his eyes fixed on the maroon streaks coursing down the guards' leg.

There was blood, lots of blood. And then he saw where the bullet entered. The tearing of the flesh and the jagged edges of the wound made Brandon's bloated stomach curdle. He resisted the urge to relieve the pressure from bile rising up in his throat. Instead, he drew his eyes away from the wound and tried to focus on helping the guard.

Releasing the dull striped tie from his neck, Brandon wrapped it around Leah's leg, just underneath the gaping wound to try and stave off the spillage of blood. Leah winced from the pressure shooting up from her leg.

"What the hell happened here," Officer Myers shouted; winded from his jaunt around the building. He'd been battling money hungry people in the front of the bank, claiming handfuls of money that spilled from the ATM when he heard a gunshot sound off around the building. He ran around to see what the disturbance was, and potentially apprehend the suspects when his search drew him to the back of the building.

"She's been shot," Brandon replied. "Get me some help back here!"

"Can you get me up off the ground," Leah asked.

The two men looked at each other and went into action. Brandon lifted his weight from the ground with a groan and positioned himself on one side while Officer Myers got on the other. Gently, each man lifted one of Leah's arms onto his shoulders. She groaned again. With another visual check-in, Brandon counted it off.

"One, two..." and on three, both men hoisted Leah to a standing position. She whimpered when her position changed. Officer Myers shot Leah a sympathetic look. Unable to put any weight on her injured leg, the two men placed their free hand under Leah's thighs and lifted her again into a sitting position. The pressure was too much and Leah cried out again. In tandem, the men turned her and then carried Leah back to the building. The jaunt was longer than expected as the back door automatically closed and locked and neither of the men had their keycard to open it. They had to carry Leah around the side of the building to get her through the front door. People still milled around, hoping more money would spew from the machine. Seeing the injured guard caused some to pause, but not all. One man was helpful enough to open the front door so Leah's rescuers could get her into the building.

New sirens behind them alerted to the police and ambulance showing on scene. Officer Myers had made the call once Leah was safely positioned in a chair. Within minutes, the bank lobby was filled with New York's finest securing the scene.

EMT's were directed to Leah and attended to her. Leah was grateful even though it still hurt like hell. The medical technician's took her vital signs and inspected her wound. They had some baseline questions about what happened, but nothing too in-depth. That would be the policeman's job. Theirs was to get her stable enough to be transported to the hospital. Leah remembered to respond as guard Sarah Middleton without hesitation. She tensed every time somebody touched her injured leg and fought back real tears when the touch was too intense. It would be easy to be preoccupied with her own discomfort, but Leah's thoughts were much further away.

Chapter Twenty Two

"Hey, there's something going on down at Atlantic Bank of New York. You wanna go check it out?"

Brittany was far too enthusiastic for Mason. He didn't even bother looking up from the file he'd been reading to acknowledge her presence as she plopped her ass on the corner of his desk.

"Hey! I'm talking to you," Brittany persisted; flipping the cover on the file and closing it. Mason didn't miss a beat. Instead of the reaction she so desperately desired, Mason opened the file again and continued to review.

"Are you really going to keep doing this?"

Mason had been icing Brittany since she pushed up on him in the parking lot. Brittany didn't like it although his response should have been expected.

"Fine then," Brittany spat. "I'll go check it out myself." Brittany lifted herself from the desk but not before ensuring that she leaned in and brushed up against Mason. His abrupt recoil was another slap to her heart. Mason wished it was a slap to her face.

"Who knows? It might be your girl," Brittany said snidely. "Up to her old tricks again."

Brittany sauntered off. Mason didn't look up to see how hard she swayed her hips in hopes of drawing his attention. But now his interest was piqued. It didn't take long for Mason to pull up details of the burglary at Atlantic Bank of New York. It was all over the newsfeed. The FBI hadn't officially been called in so operating as an agent would be ill advised. However, he could just happen to be in the neighborhood and just happen to show up at the bank to get the details the news reporters didn't have. Grabbing his keys and jacket, Mason made his way through the building to the parking lot. Maybe it was his girl after all.

Although there had been some laughs and distance, tensions were still high between Nia, Brooklyn, and Symone. Once the van was safely tucked away in the warehouse they used from time to time, all three climbed out with duffle bags in tow.

"Was the bank transfer successful," Symone sniped, tossing the duffle she carried on the long rectangular table that sat in the middle of the room.

"Yeah, I watched it go through," Brooklyn replied, sitting her bags down as well.

"Well, at least something went right," Symone sniped again, with her hands on her hips. She was still huffy and worried. They hadn't received a call from Leah, and that was stressing everybody out.

"Dammit, Symone," Brooklyn yelled; her voice boomeranging off the vacancy in the building. "I feel bad enough about having to shoot Leah, not to mention my damn sister is being held by a motherfuckin' nut case. I don't need this shit from you!"

Symone knew she pushed too far, but she couldn't help it. Her anxiety turned outward. That's how she handled things. It was Nia who was the voice of reason.

"You both need to stop, for real. We don't have time for this."

"You're right, Nia," Brooklyn chimed in. "Symone, fuck you if you can't get with this, but I'm getting my sister back, and Leah is going to call... I just know it."

Nia fingered the duffle bags on the table.

"If the transfer was successful, what are we going to do with this? Legend asked for seventy. We've got a little more than that."

"Legend didn't ask for anything," Symone corrected. "He demanded."

Nia shot Brooklyn a gaze that was equally returned. Even though Nia tried her damndest to be reasonable, they were both getting sick of Symone at this point.

Talking about the business of it was just what Brooklyn needed to reel her emotions back in. *Focus on the work*, is what she said to herself as she unzipped one of the bags. Symone was still standing away from the table; still unwilling to let it go and be useful.

"Legend demanded seventy million. With this take, we can put it towards the property and maybe even have some to try and bail out the company," Brooklyn began. "It all depends."

Nia nodded her understanding. As she fingered the stacks of vacuum pressed bundles, she raised a question.

"I know this isn't a part of the original plan, but I can't help worrying about the court case coming up for James," Nia began sheepishly. "Do you think we can spare some of this money to hire an attorney? I mean, if something were to happen and they took James from us..."

Nia's voice cracked and her eyes clouded with tears. Both Symone and Brooklyn heard the pain she felt.

"We can do that," Symone said.

"James belongs to all of us," Brooklyn agreed. "He ain't going nowhere."

To hear her friends be so unselfish in this moment, with so much going on, touched Nia. The tears that teetered on her eyelids fell as she closed her eyes, appreciative of the women who meant so much to her.

"Thank you..."

The moment of bonding between the three women lingered as they counted up the money from the bank. But just as those thoughts played on their hearts, each one had her mind somewhere else; yet, those private thoughts remained unspoken. After the money was counted, it was time. Brooklyn made the call. She placed it on speaker phone so the others could hear.

"I need to speak to my sister."

"I need my money," Legend clapped back.

Brooklyn could feel her pulse racing and venom rising in her spirit. Hearing his voice again was a brutally painful reminder for Nia.

"Proof of life."

The phone muffled as if Legend placed his hand over it and then the line cleared.

"Hey, Brook."

Relief was instant.

"Hey, Drew."

Unexpectedly, Brooklyn choked up. She didn't realize just how much she missed her sister, and to hear her on the other end of the phone reinforced the bond the two had. But Brooklyn didn't crack. Shaking her head vigorously, she cleared the emotional cobwebs. There would be time for tears, but this wasn't it.

"You good?"

"I'm good," Drew replied. Legend stood as close to her as he possibly could, listening to every word exchanged between the two. Drew kept her emotions in check as well. She knew Legend lived to see her frightened and scared for her life. He was a sadist. Drew refused to give him the satisfaction.

"You know I'm coming for you, right?"

"I know."

Having heard enough, Legend snatched the phone from Drew's hand.

"You got your proof. Where's my money?" Legend demanded.

"We got it," Brooklyn bit back. Nia and Symone were tuned into the conversation.

"Tonight. 10 p.m. High Bridge."

Before Brooklyn had a chance to acknowledge the location, the line disconnected. That was it. The exchange was set.

Chapter Twenty Three

Brooklyn and Drew's House

"It's 9:00," Brooklyn announced.

She felt Symone's eyes on her.

"What the hell is the problem now," Brooklyn sighed. There was never a good time for Symone's brooding bullshit, and this certainly was not it.

"I don't think she should go," Symone whispered. The two were in the kitchen while Nia sat quietly at the dining room table.

For the first time in quite a while, Brooklyn and Symone were on the same page.

"I'm cool with her not going, but I need to know you have my back on this, Symone."

Symone's natural instinct was to pop off, with her loyalties being questioned. But this time, Symone restrained her instinctual predilection and took into account what Brooklyn was going through.

"Listen, I love Drew like a sister," Symone began. "Believe it or not, Brooklyn, I love you, too. I have and will always have your back... no matter how much you piss me off."

Symone looked to Brooklyn. Brooklyn saw sincerity.

"Whateva man," Brooklyn shot back; leaning her shoulder against Symone. At least for the moment, some of the tension between the two settled down.

"So did you ladies kiss and make up," Nia asked as she crossed into the kitchen.

"You know damn well Symone doesn't know how to apologize," Brooklyn chuckled.

"From what I remember, she sure doesn't," Nia chimed in.

"So, shouldn't we be leaving about now," Nia asked as the three ladies stood around the breakfast bar.

Brooklyn and Symone fell quiet; one waiting for the other to break the news to Nia. The silence was awkward, and Nia watched each of them avoiding eye contact with her.

"You don't want me to go do you?" The challenge in Nia's voice was clear.

"I don't think you're ready," Brooklyn replied.

"Me either," Symone agreed. Feeling the need to soften the blow, Symone continued. "You've been a big help so far, Nia, but Brooklyn and I can handle this part."

"So you have already decided, right? I don't get a say?"

Nia placed both hands firmly on the countertop and waited for their response.

No one said a word.

"Oh, so it's not about me not being able to help with Drew," Nia scathed. "This is about Legend. You two don't think I can handle seeing him."

"No, we don't," Symone answered. "So let us handle this. We'll bring Drew back and it will be all good."

"Hmm, okay," Nia scoffed. "Since you too have already decided what I can and cannot handle, then it doesn't matter what I say."

Nia turned and walked away.

"It's 9:15."

"We gotta go."

Drew watched Legend, unsettled and antsy. He'd been that way since the call from Brooklyn.

"For a man that's about to get everything he wants, you sure don't look happy about it."

Legend looked over to where Drew was sitting casually and comfortably on the couch. She didn't look the least bit frightened or concerned like she knew something he didn't. Drew's calm demeanor wasn't lost on him, nor was his hand-wringing and pacing lost on her. Legend forced a smile as a feeble attempt to rein it in. Drew was right. He should be cool.

"Naw," Legend said. "Just working out some things in my head, like how I'm gone spend this money."

"Mmhmm," Drew rebuffed. "If those lies you tell yourself help you sleep better at night."

Legend looked at Drew more intently; taking her in from head to toe. She was nothing like Nia, nothing at all. Maybe making the exchange wasn't the right move after all. Legend dropped the thought from his mind, and looked at the clock slightly above Drew's head.

"Let's go."

"I'm ready when you are, poppy," Drew said slickly.

Lifting herself from the couch, Drew sauntered over to where Legend stood. He still hadn't made a move toward the door. Drew brushed up on him, pausing briefly.

"I thought you were smarter than this."

Her closeness piqued him in more ways than Legend cared to reveal. Her scent lingered and he followed it, watching the sway of Drew's hips as she moved towards the door. Grabbing the keys from the side table and his piece from the small drawer, Legend slid the gun in the back of his jeans. Drew didn't see it. She was already standing by the car. Locking up, Legend popped the lock on his truck and the two climbed in. It was only then Drew got her first glance of the weapon.

"What's that all about," Drew asked coolly.

"Just in case," Legend replied, starting the truck and illuminating the headlights.

"You won't need it," Drew answered back as she reached for her seatbelt.

"Like I said, just in case."

The ride to the exchange location was quiet between captive and captor. Legend didn't like the unsettled feeling he had in his gut. Legend kept looking to his right, checking Drew, who continued to be way too calm, cool and collected.

'Never let 'em see you sweat'. That's what Drew focused on. It was something her father said to her when she was little. "Never let 'em see you sweat, baby girl," her dad would say any time the pressures of being a kid or even an adult got to be too much. Legend didn't know it, but that's what kept Drew from completely losing it; that and the fact that she knew Brooklyn would move heaven and earth to get her back. Legend was an easy man to play with. All the attraction Drew felt for him when Legend was a mysterious stranger hadn't been completely replaced with feelings of loathing and disdain. Drew still thought Legend was sexy as hell; but the overdose of psychotic tendencies kept Drew from acting on the physical and thinking about how mentally fucked up Legend had to be.

The ride for Brooklyn and Symone was equally as quiet. The two temporarily resolved their differences because they both understood the importance of this moment. Brooklyn was not her typical self. When things were stressful for her, Brooklyn intellectualized. Numbers, logic, critical thinking, all those things made sense to her. They were practical, predictable, proven even. But this? There was no practicality, no logical reasoning, no equation or problem to solve. This with Drew being taken was all emotion. This was something Brooklyn couldn't critically think her way out of or reason away. This was raw, pure, unadulterated emotion; feelings Brooklyn couldn't ever remember experiencing at this level. Even though their parents were none the wiser about this situation, Brooklyn felt all the big sister guilt of letting their parents down by not protecting Drew from this.

Yeah, it was a quiet ride, but that didn't make it any less intense.

Chapter Twenty Four

Ever since the girls left her at the house, Nia had been agitated. They underestimated her like Legend did; told her she wasn't good enough, like Legend did; made her feel inadequate like Legend did; pissed her off, just like Legend did. When Nia was trapped with her tormentor, she didn't have the wherewithal or the fortitude to strike out against what agitated her, well, not in the beginning. So just like then, Nia sat in the middle of the couch with her feet tucked under and rocked back and forth, like a child trying to soothe herself. At first, Nia rocked fast; forward and back, forward and back. Then as she thought things through, flashing to memories of her time with Legend, Nia's rock slowed and she rhythmically rocked as if there was internal music in her head that only she could hear.

The other girls had no idea about who Legend was, who he really was. They didn't have an opportunity to meet him before things went so horribly wrong. The other's also had no idea how much in love Nia was with the man who stole her heart, and then her freedom. Nia allowed her mind to go back, before the entrapment, before the pain and anguish. As she rocked, a slight smile creased her previously tight lips as she remembered Legend.

Much like any young woman, Nia wanted to feel loved, be loved by a man. Sure, she had the love of family and friends that sustained her through her younger life, but entering into womanhood, Nia wanted to experience romantic love. And in walked Legend. It was a chance encounter, nothing special or spectacular. Nia was out shopping for groceries, he caught her eye, they exchanged glances, he smiled, they chatted and exchanged phone numbers. That was it; hardly the stuff romance novels are made of. But, one phone call led to many late nights of phone calls that lasted until the wee hours of the morning while still feeling like the call lasted just minutes. And it didn't take long before the two were absolutely in love with each other. Legend was Nia's first. Her love for him deepened. And things were great. Legend was everything Nia ever thought a man in her life could be.

And when she found out they were pregnant, Nia was so excited to tell him. Her family might not be excited about Nia getting pregnant while unmarried but none of that mattered to her. Nia was carrying a child crafted in love. Excitedly, she shared the news with Legend, knowing he would be equally as excited to move on with their life together as a family. She wasn't asking for marriage; that was just a piece of paper that legitimized their relationship to the rest of the world. All Nia wanted was the man that she loved, the father of her child to be there.

The slow rocking started to accelerate again as Nia was overcome with emotion. Nia met Legend at the door grinning from ear to ear. After greeting him with a warm hug and a sensuous kiss, Legend asked what she could be so excited about.

"We're pregnant," Nia exclaimed, overjoyed.

Nia's toothy smile was quickly met with a brutal backhand to the face and five fingers clamping tightly around her throat. Her eyes widened as oxygen was short circuited and Nia's smile evaporated into a rounded gasp for the little air Legend allowed her. Nia's eyes found Legend's. Where there was once love and acceptance, Nia only saw hate and rejection. Legend's eyes were as large as hers but for different reasons. Legend's jaw clenched and a vein down the center of his forehead pulsed prominently. As his fingers closed tighter around Nia's throat, she scratched and clawed trying to keep Legend for completely shutting off her air supply. A low guttural growl came from Legend. With teeth bared, he lifted Nia. She had to tip toe to maintain contact with a hard surface.

Nia wanted to plead with her lover; ask him why he was doing this to her, but no words could be spoken. She would need air for that. Tears fell down Nia's cheeks as she groped for relief. And when Legend finally decided to let her go, he did so forcefully, using his free hand to push her away as he released his death-grip on her neck. Nia gasped hard and the new air moving down her throat caused her to choke. Legend stood over her, lauded over her; still not speaking any real words. When Nia was finally able to speak, she only had one question.

"Why?"

The question came out jagged and broken, just like her spirit. But Nia needed to understand Legend's harsh response. He'd never treated her that way before. So she waited; looking up into his downcast eyes for understanding.

Legend's chest rose and fell, swole and receded like he'd been running a race. His fists were clenched tightly by his sides and he glared at Nia as though she disgusted him.

"Why, Legend, please, tell me, why?"

And only after elongated moments of silence from him and sobs from her did Legend speak.

"I can ask you the same thing."

Nia stopped rocking. Her eyes tightened into a slither. The memory was painful, true enough, but what followed made this incident pale in comparison. Legend was never the same with Nia after that. He was cold, distant, hateful. The pregnancy she tried to hide from her family, Nia had to hide from Legend. She clung to the false hope that as her belly grew, Legend would soften, knowing it was his germ of life that swelled inside her willing womb. And when Nia found out it was a boy, she was sure that would soften Legend's cold heart. To have a son, his own son, a namesake surely would make Legend proud. Sadly for Nia, he was not.

When the baby was born, Legend was nowhere to be found. Sure, her family was there; having made peace with the fact that Nia was having a baby, whether they liked it or not.

"Have you decided on a name?"

That was a natural question. And Nia had considered a name for her son. As she looked down into the babies face, noting features that looked like his fathers, Nia longed to bestow upon her son the name of his father. And then she remembered how hurtful he was, how much pain he caused, and the hate she saw over and over in his eyes. Nia didn't want to saddle her son with the potential of that kind of legacy. She wanted her son to have his own identity as that of his father's was tarnished.

And she named him, James.

The rocking started again, not slowly but swiftly as flashes of her past popped into Nia's mind. Things were never the same between her and Legend. He treated her like he didn't want her but at the same time, wouldn't let her go. Legend threatened everything and everyone around Nia every time she got the gumption to stand up to him. When he threatened to snuff out the life of his own son, that's when Nia had to do everything in her power to protect James. Her family didn't know why she left her baby, but Nia did it to save James' life. Legend made her choose. He made her pick. The more Nia thought about that, the more she contemplated how unfair that was to her and her baby, the faster she rocked. Legend made her pick. Legend made her choose.

Tears poured from Nia's eyes as she relived those pain filled moments. The smug look on Legend's face when she returned to him empty handed, with no baby in tow. But Nia had been strong before. She summoned all her courage and risked it all to steal away from Legend. And now he was back, tormenting her family in the way he promised.

Nia jumped up off the couch. She refused to be sidelined again, not when it came to the man who denied her motherhood and made her feel so unworthy. Nia's eyes darted around and her feet moved in the direction her eyes carried her. When they landed on the object of her desire, Nia moved in earnest. Grabbing the set of car keys, Nia bolted for the garage door. Since Brooklyn and Symone rode together, there was still a car left. As Nia climbed in the driver's seat and turned the ignition, she made a decision.

Legend eased his car to the appointed location and put it in park. Dimming the headlights, Legend looked around the area tracking any movement. He was so close to getting everything he wanted and Legend didn't want anything to mess that up. This could all be a set-up, for real; if Drew's folks called the cops or something. So Legend was on high alert. Drew had been quiet the entire ride, but now sitting and waiting for her rescue, it was hard keeping her real feelings in check.

"I'll be glad when this shits over," Drew mused. "My family is going through too much right now to have to fuck with you."

Drew looked out of the passenger side window as she continued, speaking aloud, and not particularly to Legend.

"And to think I almost fell for your trifling ass..." Drew looked in Legend's direction and turned up her lip. "...my nephew is going to know how to treat women and be about something," Drew mumbled. Thoughts of James and the upcoming court hearing came to Legend's mind. The girls didn't know that while they thought they'd disconnected the call during one of their conversation's the day before, the line had been open and Legend heard everything.

Headlights in the distance drew both of their attention. Peering over the dashboard, Drew was hopeful, and nervous. As the car slowed and came to a stop, Legend reached for his gun. His movement made Drew look in his direction.

"Come on, man," Drew bargained.

"Like I said, just in case," Legend replied as he shoved the gun in the back of his waistband.

"You won't need it," Drew continued.

"Don't give me a reason, Drew," Legend warned. "You do everything I tell you and we won't have a problem. Understand?"

"Yeah, I understand."

Legend turned his attention back to the car, now parked directly in front of his. He squinted his eyes as the headlights blared through the windshield.

Brooklyn and Symone were ready; as ready as they could ever be. Brooklyn needed visual confirmation that her sister was alright. Seeing two heads in the car across from them made it clear that Drew was there. Brooklyn had been contemplating the best course of action as far as transferring the money to the lowlife that held Drew captive. She didn't think Legend was dumb enough to go for the cash in the duffle bags. It was well short of the 70 million he demanded. So this would be a wire transfer, account to account. The faster the better. Symone had been in deep thought as well; how to get her family out of this situation without giving Legend a dime. It would be easy to contact Mason and let him do his whole FBI sting thing. Symone knew that was impractical although she would love to see Legend's ass handcuffed and locked behind bars. Mason would intervene on her behalf, of that Symone was sure. But there would be too many questions she couldn't afford to answer without implicating herself or the other girls.

Brooklyn and Symone waited until they saw movement from the other car. Their eyes were fixed on Legend as he exited the driver side, walked around the back of the vehicle and opened the door to the passenger side. When Drew stepped out, both girls breathed a huge sigh of relief.

"She looks ok, right," Brooklyn asked, seeking reassurance that her eyes were not deceiving her.

"She looks good, Brooklyn," Symone affirmed.

"Okay, let's get this done."

With that Brooklyn and Symone stepped out of their vehicle and closed the doors behind them. The sound echoed against the vastness of the space underneath the bridge. But no one moved forward. It was like each was waiting for the other to make the first decisive move. Legend grabbed Drew by the arm. When she snatched away, it pissed him off and when he grabbed her arm the second time, he held it tightly.

"Bastard," Drew spat, resenting his touch; after craving it for so long.

Legend was tired of the games. As he stepped forward, he marched Drew forward in front of him. He didn't want to expose himself completely just in case anyone had any bright ideas. It was only then that Brooklyn and then Symone moved forward.

"Drew, you good," Brooklyn called out over the space between them.

"Yeah sis, I'm good," Drew replied coolly. Inside she was glad to see her family but she didn't let it show.

"How you want to do this Legend," Brooklyn asked, directing her attention towards Drew's captor.

"You got my money?"

"Would we be here if we didn't," Brooklyn replied testily.

"Let me see it," Legend barked back.

...this motherfucker here, Brooklyn thought to herself. Clearly she would have to take the lead to make the exchange. It was clear Legend hadn't completely thought this through.

"What did you expect, bags of cash," Brooklyn challenged, not waiting for a response. "This will be a wire transfer. Simple and clean."

"Let's do it then," Legend responded anxiously.

"All we need is your account number Legend and we can get this done," Symone chimed in.

"Bring Drew to the middle. Give me the account number. When the money transfers, you let her go," Brooklyn instructed.

"Done," Legend called back.

Both groups moved, closing the distance between them. Now Brooklyn could see Drew clearly. She looked okay. There was a slight smile that spread across Drew's lips that convinced Brooklyn that it was all going to be alright. Legend looked between both women, not trusting either of them. He held his grip firmly on Drew and his free hand flirted with the butt of his gun. Symone watched Legend closely. He'd proven he wasn't trustworthy. When she saw his hand behind his back, Symone warned Brooklyn.

"Watch him," she whispered. Brooklyn paid closer attention to his posture.

Slowly pulling her cell phone up so Legend could see it, Brooklyn requested the account number.

"451," Legend called out. "309..."

Peeling tires screeching against the gravel caught everyone's attention. Bright lights flashed from a direction they shouldn't have been. The speeding car was heading straight for Drew and Legend.

"Oh shit," Legend screamed as the car bore down on the pair. As he reached in his waistband to retrieve his gun, Drew took his moment of inattentiveness to snatch away from him. She broke in the direction of her sister running full speed. And then everything seemed to move in slow motion. Brooklyn grabbed Drew. Symone watched the car moving in on Legend. When the lights passed her eyes, she could see Nia behind the wheel.

"No, Nia, No!"

Did he hear what he thought he heard? There was no time to consider. The car was aiming straight for him. Legend pulled the gun up, leveling it at the windshield of the car. The car continued to accelerate.

Legend shot off two shots in quick succession, shattering the glass of the oncoming car. Nia ducked lower behind the steering wheel. Through cracked glass she kept her target in sight. Drew, Brooklyn and Symone watched, shocked at what was going on.

They called out to her but Nia couldn't hear them.

"Nia! No! Stop! Nia!"

There was a moment when she considered what she was doing; when Nia thought about all the love and pain the man in front of her caused. Nia's eyes tightened and she pressed hard on the gas pedal.

"This is for James..."

Nia closed her eyes at the moment of impact.

To be continued…

Author's Note

Thank you so much for reading the first installment of Prowl! We hope you enjoyed it and plan to continue along with this crazy bunch of characters! Reviews are the life blood of independent writers. The more reviews we get, the more Amazon and others promote the book. If you want to see more Prowl, a review would go a long way towards allowing me to write more books. If you liked the book, we ask you to write a review of Prowl Book 1 on Amazon.com, Goodreads or where ever you go for your book information. Thank you so much. Doing so means a lot to us. If you didn't like the book, then please disregard this paragraph.

More Books by Deidra D. S. Green

- **The Twisted Sister Trilogy**
- Twisted Sister (book 1)
- Twisted's Revenge (Book 2)
- After the Twist (Book 3)
- **Woman at the Top of the Stairs Trilogy**

- Woman at the Top of the Stairs (Book 1)
- Sweetest Revenge (Book 2)
- The Final Say (Book 3)
- Suddenly Single: So Undeserving
- **The Chloe Daniel's Mysteries**
- Sick, Sicker, Sickest: (The 1st installment in the Chloe Daniels Mysteries)
- HUSH: (The 2nd installment in Chloe Daniels)
- Mischief's Mayhem: (The 3rd installment in Chloe Daniels)
- FIT: (The 4th Installment in Chloe Daniels)
- RUN (the 5th installment in Chloe Daniels)
- Ivy: Some Say she's Poison
- Interstate 64
- My Guy Friday
- Elite Affairs I: Orchestrated Beauty
- Elite Affairs II: Simple Elegance

Check out Deidra's Amazon page
amzn.to/2nqi3iG

Grab a personalized copy at
bit.ly/readwithDDSG

Get a free e-book when you subscribe to Deidra's newsletter!
https://www.instafreebie.com/free/Vev7x

More Books by Stephanie Nicole Norris

Contemporary Romance

- Everything I Always Wanted (A Friends to Lovers Romance)
- Safe With Me (Falling for a Rose Book One)

Romantic Suspense Thrillers

- Beautiful Assassin
- Beautiful Assassin 2 Revelations
- Mistaken Identity
- Trouble In Paradise
- Vengeful Intentions (Trouble In Paradise 2)
- For Better and Worse (Trouble In Paradise 3)
- Until My Last Breath (Trouble In Paradise 4)

Christian Romantic Suspense

- Broken
- Reckless Reloaded

Crime Fiction

- Prowl
- Hidden (Coming Soon)

Fantasy

- Golden (Rapunzel's F'd Up Fairytale)

Non-Fiction

- Against All Odds (Surviving the Neonatal Intensive Care Unit) *Non-Fiction

Made in the USA
Middletown, DE
19 October 2022